Lip Reading

Maybe she really is mad at me, Jake wondered. But for what? He racked his brain for some memory of something he might have done.

"Look, I'm really sorry," Jake blurted out.

Now it was Nancy's turn to give him a strange look. "What for?"

Jake shrugged. "I don't know. For whatever I did wrong."

Nancy laughed gleefully. "I don't know what you're talking about, but I love you." She grabbed the collar of his coat and kissed him hard on the mouth. "Now get back to your study carrel and be brilliant. I have work to do!"

Jake headed back out into the night, more confused than ever. . . .

NANCY DREW ON CAMPUS™

Available from ARCHWAY Paperbacks

Nancy Drew
on campus ™ # 14

Hard to Get

Carolyn Keene

AN ARCHWAY PAPERBACK
Published by POCKET BOOKS
New York London Toronto Sydney Tokyo Singapore

AN ARCHWAY PAPERBACK *Original*

An Archway Paperback published by
POCKET BOOKS, a division of Simon & Schuster Inc.
1230 Avenue of the Americas, New York, NY 10020

Copyright © 1996 by Simon & Schuster Inc.
Produced by Mega-Books, Inc.

ISBN: 0-671-56803-5

First Archway Paperback printing October 1996

10 9 8 7 6 5 4 3 2 1

NANCY DREW, AN ARCHWAY PAPERBACK and colophon are registered trademarks of Simon & Schuster Inc.

NANCY DREW ON CAMPUS is a trademark of Simon & Schuster Inc.

Cover photos by Pat Hill Studio

Printed in the U.S.A.

IL 8+

Hard to Get

CHAPTER 1

Jake, over here!" Nancy Drew cried, waving at her boyfriend, Jake Collins. After breaking through the crowd of Wilder University students gathered on the field of Holliston Stadium, Jake reached out and pulled Nancy into his arms.

"Hi, Nan," Jake said, looking flushed and happy.

"Hi, yourself." Nancy smiled. "It's about time you got here. The entire student body is at this pep rally. You wouldn't want to be the only one on campus to miss it, would you?"

"Of course not," Jake answered. "Especially not if it means missing out on seeing you." The crowd roared, and Nancy stood on tiptoe to watch the Wilder University football squad race out from under the goalpost at one end of the huge stadium. As the team members were each introduced, she and Jake cheered for them with everyone else.

This was the biggest pep rally of the year. In less than eighteen hours, the Wilder U. Norsemen would be kicking off against their arch-rivals, Coldwater State. The cheerleaders formed a pyramid in the middle of the field as the marching band followed them onto the field.

Paul Cody walked up behind Nancy and Jake. "Hey, I know you two. You're just here for the free coffee, right?"

Nancy laughed. "You bet. Where do we get it?" She playfully hooked one of her arms through Paul's and pretended to drag him off the field. Nancy knew Paul was probably missing his girlfriend, one of Nancy's best friends, Bess Marvin. Bess had had to pass on the pep rally because of a rehearsal for a series of one-act plays the Wilder Drama Department was putting on.

Before Nancy could say anything more to Paul, she heard a familiar laugh close by and turned to see her other best friend, George Fayne, with George's roommate, Pam Miller. Both had on heavy sweatshirts and winter running tights.

"Come on, it's not that cold," George was saying to Pam. "Anyway, here come the guys with hot coffee," George added as her boyfriend, Will Blackfeather, and Pam's boyfriend, Jamal Lewis, joined them. "Now *that* should get your blood flowing."

Nancy scanned the packed field. Wilder University sweatshirts and heads in woolly hats were everywhere. She spotted Reva Ross, one of her suitemates from Thayer Hall, weaving across the field through mobs of students.

"Hi, guys," Reva called out as she and her boyfriend, Andy Rodriguez, joined them. "Anyone seen Eileen?"

"Nope. But she told me she was meeting Emmet here," Nancy said. "Maybe they met and took off somewhere."

"Wishful thinking." Shaking her head, Reva nodded toward the knot of football players and their girlfriends standing nearby. Emmet Lehman was with them, but Eileen O'Connor was nowhere in sight.

Nancy noticed that Emmet was searching the crowd, too. "Looks like he's still waiting."

"Eileen's nervous about seeing him again," Reva confided.

"I know," Nancy said.

Emmet was Paul Cody's roommate in Zeta House, and he and Eileen had been set up by their friends on a blind date. Nancy knew that they had gotten off to a pretty rocky start on their first date. Eileen told her suitemates that she was definitely attracted to him, but that she was worried about whether they were too different to get along. Emmet was totally into sports, and even though Eileen was on the crew team, she was mainly into painting and sculpture.

Oh well, Nancy thought, if they're meant to be

a couple, they'll work it out. She turned to Jake and planted a kiss on his cheek.

"What was that for?" he asked, startled. "Not that I'm complaining, mind you."

"Because I'm so excited for you. When are you going to spill the beans to the rest of your friends?" Nancy stood back, staring into his eyes. "If you don't say something soon, I'll do it myself."

Will eyed him curiously. "What's up?"

Nancy grinned. "Jake's got fantastic news. Come on, tell them."

"Okay, okay," Jake said. "Remember that article I wrote for the *Wilder Times* about the white supremacist group on campus?"

"Ugh, even the mention of those racist creeps makes me feel queasy," Pam said. A number of African-American students, including Pam and Jamal, had been hassled by a group of local racist skinheads whose organization had appeared on campus a few weeks earlier. Jake had written an exposé on the group.

"Sorry," Pam said. "What about the article?"

"It's been picked up by the *Chicago Daily Herald*." Jake grinned shyly.

"The *Herald!* That's a national newspaper!" George cried.

Will clapped him on the back. "You're famous, man!"

"I guess it is pretty great," Jake admitted.

"He's not just Wilder's star reporter anymore,"

Nancy teased. She beamed as she watched Jake accept congratulations from their friends.

Jake was the crack reporter for the campus newspaper, the *Wilder Times,* and Nancy knew he had dreams of writing for a major city newspaper. She felt sure that he'd fulfill them.

"Hey, you guys, they're building a bonfire." Pam pointed to the far end of the field. "Let's get down there."

Nancy hung back as Jake and the others started moving down the field. She pulled George and Will aside. "Listen," she said, lowering her voice and talking quickly. "I was thinking of throwing Jake a surprise celebration party next week."

Will was nodding his head. "Great idea."

"Wednesday would be perfect," Nancy continued excitedly. "Everyone will be done with exams by then."

"Wait a minute, Nan," George cut in. "Didn't you just tell me how much work you have in the next few days?"

"I know," Nancy admitted. "But it's just a Western Civ paper and a couple of exams. Not every teacher is giving them."

"But the ones you will have are only twenty-five percent of your entire grade," George reminded her.

"Well, this is too exciting not to celebrate," Nancy said. "Jake deserves it, and I'm going to pull it off—exams or no exams!"

* * *

"Earth to Eileen."

Eileen blinked, snapping out of her daydream. She was sitting on the couch in the lounge of Thayer Hall's suite 301, wearing the same sweats she'd had on all afternoon while she studied at the Rock, Wilder's library.

Pictures of Emmet Lehman had been drifting through her brain. Basically, Eileen was trying to decide what it was that made her want to see him again. They'd talked so little on their date, she didn't really know what he was like. Eileen knew she liked the way he looked, but that was about all so far. She just wasn't sure if she should pursue this relationship.

"Oh, hi, Dawn," Eileen said.

Dawn Steiger, the suite's resident advisor, was standing over her in an oversize brown wool sweater, her luxurious blond hair flowing out from under a stocking cap.

"I thought you were meeting Emmet at the rally," Dawn said.

"I was."

"Something wrong?" Dawn tugged off her hat and perched on the arm of the couch.

Eileen shrugged sadly. "No, not really."

"You're not getting along?"

Eileen blew a stray hair out of her eyes. "I can't tell." She shrugged. "We really haven't spent any time together."

"So what's the problem?"

Eileen looked up at Dawn. "To be honest, cold

6

feet. Wouldn't it be *awful* if things didn't work out?"

"What would really be awful," Dawn said, "is if you don't give it a try. I saw Emmet when he came by to pick you up the other night. I thought he was really cute."

Eileen couldn't help smiling. "He is, isn't he."

"He was o-*kay*," came a voice from out in the hall. "If you like that type, that is."

Eileen grimaced. "Hi, Stephanie."

Stephanie sauntered into the lounge in worn blue jeans and a clingy long-sleeve shirt. With her long black hair carefully tossed to give it a windblown look, she could have stepped out of a jeans ad in a magazine.

"So what type *is* Emmet?" Eileen asked.

Eileen caught the threatening, don't-you-dare glare that Dawn threw Stephanie's way.

"Adorable," Dawn cut in quickly.

"Though football players are usually so deadly *dull*," Stephanie criticized.

"Not all athletes are alike," Dawn pointed out. "That's just a myth."

Stephanie motioned Eileen closer and lowered her voice to a conspiratorial whisper: "You should do what I do. Get them to take you to the fanciest places, make them pay for everything, then when they disappoint you, it won't be a *complete* waste of your time."

Dawn rolled her eyes. "Stephanie Keats's guide to eternal happiness. Look, Eileen, if I were you I'd give Emmet a chance. Go meet him at the rally. What do you have to lose?"

"Dawn's right," Stephanie said, her mouth curling up in a smile. "You don't have anything to lose."

"Thanks a lot," Eileen replied, shooting Stephanie an annoyed glance. Then she sighed. "Okay. I'll go." She looked up at Stephanie. "And since you think going is such a good idea, you're coming with me."

Stephanie looked horrified. "A pep rally? *Moi?*"

"What else do you have to do tonight?" Dawn asked.

"Tons!" Stephanie started to say, then paused, as if searching her brain for all of her appointments. Obviously, she couldn't come up with a single one. She peered at Eileen, defeated. "Oh, all right, but just until I hand you off to your friend."

"I'll get dressed," Eileen said, popping up.

Tugging her hat over her ears, Dawn headed for the door. "Oh," she said, turning to Stephanie. "I wanted to ask you something. There's this beautiful shirt I've had my eye on at Berrigan's, but it's a little out of my price range."

"I smell employee discount!" Eileen laughed.

Dawn smiled sheepishly at Stephanie.

Stephanie threw up her hands. "Why is it that the day I get a job at Berrigan's Department Store, I suddenly become Miss Popularity?"

Eileen poked her in the side, bringing out a smile. "Come on, don't you remember the seven hundred fifty bags I carried around for you on your recent shopping spree?"

"How can you be so ungrateful," Stephanie complained mockingly. "Don't forget about that gorgeous dress I bought you."

"I know, that was really generous of you," Eileen admitted. "And didn't it feel good to do a favor? Just think how much *better* you'll feel doing Dawn a favor, too."

Stephanie rolled her eyes. "Okay, okay. I'll think about it."

"Flight Four-eleven to Los Angeles will begin boarding in five minutes," a voice over the P.A. system in Chicago's O'Hare Airport announced.

"I bet I never told you how much I love airports," Ginny Yuen said as she hitched Ray Johansson's guitar case up on her shoulder. She was walking with her boyfriend, Ray, and the rest of his band, the Beat Poets, toward their gate. "They make me feel so free."

Ray lowered his smoldering eyes toward hers and squeezed her hand. "Me, too," he said in his quiet voice.

"You have all the papers?" Spider Kelly, one of Ray's bandmates, asked.

Ray tapped the pocket of his leather bomber jacket. "All here. Not that I understand any of that contract stuff."

9

"I keep telling you, we don't *have* to understand," Spider said. "That's what lawyers are for. My brother-in-law looked over the contract and gave us a thumbs-up."

"All I'm interested in are the little numbers after the dollar sign," Bruce Kincaid, another band member, piped up. Sam Dixon, the drummer, nodded in agreement.

"I hope they'll have security in L.A. to hold back all of our fans," Spider said.

"And limos," Denny Curtis, the bass player, added, draping an arm over Ray's shoulder. "If we're going to do lunch with the prez of Pacific Records, we need a limo, right?"

Laughing, Ray gave a double thumbs-up.

Ginny laughed, too. But she had to admit she wasn't as deliriously happy as Ray and the others. It didn't surprise her that the Beat Poets were finally getting the recognition they deserved. After all, Ray's raspy voice was hauntingly beautiful. And Spider's guitar playing was imaginative. The second she heard them, she knew they'd make it big. She had even collaborated with Ray on a few songs, songs that Pacific Records had liked the most.

It was a little overwhelming, though, how quickly everything was happening. One day Ginny and Ray were just another couple on campus. Now, suddenly, Ray and his band were being flown out to Los Angeles by a big recording label to sign a contract.

"You guys be careful out there," Ginny warned. "I know Pacific Records is excited to sign you up, but they're also out to make a lot of money off you. Don't forget it's still your music."

"Don't worry, Gin," Ray said. "They want to start us small. After everything's settled, that is. As soon as we've cut the tracks for the album, we'll start to play around at some clubs to get a fan base,"

"Yeah," Bruce cut in. "Then shoot a video."

"Then we'll have the press junket," Spider said, laughing.

"Yeah, right." Ray grinned.

Ginny squeezed Ray's hand. "I hope when you get back you'll still have time for me," she said, only half joking.

"Sure," Ray said with a mischievous twinkle in his eye. "I'll try to fit you in."

"Flight Four-eleven to L.A. boarding . . ."

Ginny kissed Ray on the cheek. "You'd better *fit in* the library," she said. "Don't forget you're still a college student. Exams are on the first three days of next week."

"Let's go, Ray!" Bruce called, heading for the gate. "See ya, Gin." He waved. Sam and Denny followed, also waving goodbye.

"We'd better go," Spider urged Ray.

Ginny handed Ray his guitar. "I miss you already."

"There's always the phone," Ray pointed out.

Ginny gazed up at him longingly. "When will you call?"

"Well," Ray began, "we have meetings all day tomorrow—"

"And tomorrow night that guy said we had to go check out some club," Spider said.

"What about Sunday?" Ray asked.

Spider shook his head. "More meetings, contract signing in the afternoon, flight home in the evening—"

Ray arched his eyebrow. "I'll try to find some time tomorrow or Sunday, but it's going to be pretty busy. Maybe I can call you from the plane," he said. "They have phones on them now, you know—"

The loud, excited feeling inside Ginny's heart suddenly quieted down. "Just don't forget to come back, okay?"

"Yeah, we'll *do* college," Spider joked. He caught Ray's eye, and they broke up laughing.

"Sure," Ginny said, straining to stay light-hearted. The fact was, Ray struggled to keep his grades up and needed to study hard. Spider was already flunking half his classes. Bruce, Sam, and Denny weren't even in college. Not exactly the most positive academic influences, Ginny knew.

Ray was smiling that wry smile of his that made Ginny melt. "Stop worrying about me," he said. "I'll be fine. I always am. If I can't call, I'll dream about you."

"Me, too," Ginny said, giving Ray one last hug.

She felt small and safe in his strong arms. But she *was* worrying. About Ray's grades. About the band. And something else about all this that was nagging her, something she couldn't put her finger on.

He always comes through, Ginny reminded herself as Ray walked away.

Just before he disappeared through the security check, Ray turned and waved.

Grinning, Ginny lifted her hand. "Go get 'em," she mouthed.

CHAPTER 2

"Okay, everybody, *excellent* job!" Alan Farber, the director of the one-acts, called out from the darkened seats of Hewlitt Auditorium. "See you Sunday afternoon."

"Whew," Bess Marvin said, stretching out in her leotard on the floodlit stage and staring up into the lights. Tugging out her scrunchie, she fluffed out her long blond hair. "That was a grueling rehearsal."

"Welcome to the wonderful world of acting," Casey Fontaine replied, sitting cross-legged next to her.

Casey, a suitemate of Nancy's, was tall, with red hair and finely chiseled good looks. Casey had been a professional actress, and the star of a hit TV show, *The President's Daughter,* before

14

starting college. At first the thought of acting on the same stage with Casey made Bess feel hopelessly inferior. But while acting together in the department's production of *Grease!,* Casey turned out to be one of Bess's biggest fans.

"Hey, Bess, that last scene of yours was really incredible. You're getting better every day."

Bess looked up at her boyishly handsome friend Brian Daglian and smiled. Another lover of the theater and acting, Brian had been a good buddy of hers since the beginning of school.

"You weren't so bad yourself," Bess said, pushing herself to her feet. "What do you guys say we grab a cup of coffee at Java Joe's, then head over to the rally."

"Rally!" Casey cried. "I'm starving. Can't we just eat instead?"

"Ditto on that," Brian chimed in. "How long have we been here, since two o'clock? And what is it now, seven?"

"I want to meet Paul for at least a few minutes," Bess explained. "And I promised Eileen I'd be there for moral support. You did, too," she reminded Casey.

"Oh, right"—Casey winced—"Eileen's big date."

"I hope this means you'll chaperon me the next time *I* go on a date," Brian quipped, popping his head through the neck of his sweater.

Bess, Casey, and Brian were halfway up the aisle when Alan Farber returned from the wings.

"One more thing, everybody!" he called. "Jeanne Glasseburg, an acting coach from the New York Institute for Dramatic Arts, will be teaching a one-time, by-invitation-only course next semester in the theater department—"

"Jeanne Glasseburg," Casey whispered excitedly to Bess. "I saw her work an improv class once. She's *amazing!*"

"Ms. Glasseburg will be scouting our acting classes over the next few weeks for participants," Alan continued. "And she'll be attending the one-act plays. But the class is limited, and from what I saw tonight, there should be stiff competition for spots. So stay focused, everybody, and break a leg!"

"Wow." Casey breathed deeply as they hit the chilly night air. "Jeanne Glasseburg has coached some of the best actors in the world. I'd love to get in a class with her."

"But you don't need it," Brian told her.

Bess nodded. "You're already a great actress. Not to mention a star."

Casey shook her head. "Wrong. You can always improve your craft. She's worked with lots of established actors and made them completely brilliant. Stardom doesn't impress her. What about you, Bess—wouldn't it be great?"

"Sure," Bess replied uncertainly. Quickening her pace to keep up with Casey, though, she felt her mind start to race.

Jeanne Glasseburg sounds just like what I

need, she thought. Someone to help me develop the talent I have . . .

Bess eyed Casey's back and sighed. With Casey and all the upperclass theater majors, she said to herself, I don't have a shot.

As the last football player was introduced and sprinted across the field through the gauntlet of cheerleaders, George sidled up to Will. "Are we going to win tomorrow? I didn't even know it was Coldwater State that Wilder was playing, until I got to the rally."

"The answer is yes," Will replied. "And just for your information, Wilder is leading the conference."

George nodded, impressed, taking in all the activities of the night. The huge bonfire was burning brightly in the end zone. The female cheerleaders had made a pyramid four high, and the male cheerleaders were doing rows of handsprings in front of the Norsemen's team mascot, a giant Viking.

"Well, *this* is fun!" George said. "Even if I haven't been paying much attention to our games lately."

"Oh, these moronic sports rituals," a voice pierced through the excited buzz of the crowd.

Stephanie, in matching sweater and hat, was striding across the football field, cheerfully aware of the group of admiring guys she left in her wake.

George groaned. Though Stephanie wasn't the witch everyone thought she was at the beginning of the semester, she still hadn't exactly made George's list of favorite people. The good news, though, was that she had Eileen with her.

"I mean, just *look* at those cheerleaders," Stephanie was saying with an ironic laugh. "They look like idiots! And the football players! They're practically prehistoric."

Emmet, who had been one of the first members of the team introduced, spotted Eileen right away and walked straight over to her. "Hey, where've you been? You missed the intros."

George sighed with relief when Eileen's face broke out in a wide grin. They do make an adorable couple, she thought.

"Studying," Eileen said.

"Lost track of the time, huh?" Emmet smiled at her.

"Hey!" George told Eileen and Emmet excitedly. "Jake got his article about the racist group into the *Chicago Herald!*"

"Excellent, Jake!" Eileen cried.

Emmet smiled, his eyes searching Eileen's face, full of curiosity and questions.

"Hey," Stephanie said, pointing at him and squinting with concentration, "aren't you in that easy geography class, the one that all the football jocks take?"

Even in the dim light George could see that

that made Emmet mad. She threw her roommate, Pam, a helpless look.

"That's Astro-lab one twelve, Stephanie," Pam corrected Stephanie. "You're a geo major, aren't you, Emmet?"

"Astrophysics, actually," Emmet replied.

Stephanie was doubtful. "Really? I'm impressed," she said. "Most football players I know can't put three sentences together."

"Stephanie!" said George.

Stephanie looked from face to face, her expression all innocence and light. "What did I say now?"

Emmet looked at her darkly. "Nothing."

"Actually, *I* played football in high school," Jake spoke up.

"Me, too," Jamal, Pam's boyfriend, tossed in. "I guess that makes me a Neanderthal."

Stephanie tried to backpedal a bit. "I didn't mean to insult anyone. Excuse me for being alive."

But it was too late. George felt bad for Emmet. Obviously, he was self-conscious about his jock image.

"I guess nothing about Wilder would look good to you these days, Stephanie," Pam shot back, "now that you have the hots for Jonathan Baur."

All eyes turned on Stephanie.

"Jonathan who?" Nancy asked dramatically.

"Oh, just some guy who works at Berrigan's," Pam explained blithely.

Pam worked part-time with Stephanie in Berrigan's cosmetics department, and she'd been coming back from work telling George stories of Stephanie's preparations for an all-out assault on their older, gorgeous floor manager.

"Not true!" Stephanie protested.

George nudged her. "That's not what I heard."

"Is that tall, dark, and handsome Number Eleven in your life, Steph?" Jake joked.

"Or slim, blond, and beautiful Number Eight?" Jamal said to everyone's laughter.

George crossed her arms. "I guess nothing at Wilder, especially of the human male variety, is mature enough for you anymore."

Stephanie shot them all pouty, injured looks.

George glanced at Emmet to see how he was taking it. He seemed to be trying to ignore Stephanie.

"So," George said cheerily, hooking her arm through Will's. "What's on the program after the pep rally tonight? Eileen, Emmet, any brilliant ideas?"

But George overheard Emmet talking softly to Eileen. "Don't worry," he said, "I've heard all that dumb-jock stuff before."

Eileen nodded understandingly. "Steph's not exactly a rocket scientist, you know," she said with a wink.

While the others were making plans, George

watched as Eileen and Emmet laughed and began to talk quietly. Stephanie's comments were obviously forgotten.

Well, good. Emmet *is* hot, George thought to herself. And it would be great to see those two get together.

"There's Paul!" Bess cried, and disappeared into the crowd at the rally.

Casey, cupping her piping hot coffee in both hands, looked but didn't see Paul anywhere. "Do *you* see him?" she asked Brian.

Everyone in the crowd seemed to be laughing and talking at once. The drum corps was playing an exceptionally loud rhythm.

Brian shook his head. "It's mayhem."

"Bess and Paul are equipped with radar for each other," Casey said. "It's like they're fated to be together."

"Just like you and Charley," Brian pointed out.

The mere mention of Charley's name made Casey smile. Charley Stern, her boyfriend, had been Casey's co-star on *The President's Daughter*. He'd stayed behind to keep working when Casey gave up the glitz of Hollywood for college. But the week before, he flew in from L.A. to propose marriage. He missed Casey so much and was so afraid of losing her, he'd wanted them to get married right away. After a lot of painful discussion, they decided to wait until Casey graduated.

"Hey there." Casey heard a familiar cry and saw Nancy waving her hand high above the crowd.

Casey and Brian snaked through and found Nancy and her crowd chatting and laughing. Eileen was standing next to a new guy Casey hadn't seen before. Bess, meanwhile, was folded in Paul's arms.

Brian laid a consoling hand on Casey's shoulder. "Do you miss Charley?"

"Some times more than others," she replied.

Every morning since they'd gotten engaged, Casey examined herself in the mirror. Though she didn't feel any different physically, she reminded herself that things were changed for good. "Mrs. Stern," she'd repeat over and over.

Though I don't feel very "Mrs." at the moment, she thought to herself as she scanned the group. Except for her and Brian, everyone else was paired off. Bess and Paul, Nancy and Jake, George and Will, Pam and Jamal, and now Eileen and the new guy.

In the back of Casey's mind, a little voice was admitting the unadmittable: Maybe it *would* be fun to have a boyfriend at school.

"Hey, Case. We really should stop meeting like this."

Nick Dimartini, Jake's roommate, was standing next to her. Tall and lean, Nick had strong features and great eyes. Lately Casey and Nick had often found themselves alone together at different parties. Once, Nick offered to walk her back to Thayer Hall, and Casey couldn't remember laughing so hard—not since she and Charley had first started dating.

"It must be destiny," Nick quipped, holding her hand and staring meaningfully into her eyes. Then he broke up laughing.

"I don't know, Nick," she said with mock seriousness. "Maybe you're right. You know what they say, 'Third time's a charm.' "

"Is this the third time?" Nick asked. "It seems like the fifth or sixth."

"Maybe we should go out sometime and make it official," Casey said before she could stop herself.

"Now, Casey," he replied with a mischievous smile, "we all know you're spoken for."

Casey sighed dramatically with mock sorrow. "I know."

She felt a sharp elbow in her side. Bess was mouthing the words "Stop flirting!"

"Remember your hunky Hollywood fiancé?" Brian whispered in her ear.

It dawned on Casey what she'd said.

Weird, she reflected, then remembered how much fun flirting used to be. In Hollywood, guys of model quality were a dime a dozen.

It was so harmless, she thought. But Charley had just asked her to marry him, and she'd just given him a yes.

Well, she rationalized, it's not as if I'm really interesting in starting anything with Nick.

Casey stole a glimpse at him.

Though he *is* incredibly attractive, she thought. If it weren't for Charley, I'd go out with him—why not?

She scanned the crowd. Good-looking guys were everywhere. And many of them were throwing her glances of their own. And what was worse, Casey didn't mind it one bit.

She swallowed hard. You already said the magic word, she thought, then whispered it under her breath, to see how it would sound: "Forever."

It sounded funny. Funny as in *strange.*

Smiling stiffly, Casey stepped forward into her group of friends, trying to distract herself. But she just couldn't shake off the feeling of being surrounded by hordes of great-looking guys. Almost all of them, she knew, available—and willing.

And she realized that it didn't feel so bad. What, she thought, is the matter with me!

"I love you," Bess spoke in Paul's ear, then pressed her mouth softly against his.

Closing his eyes, Paul hugged Bess tighter. When he'd spotted her coming toward him out of the crowd, she'd looked like a vision, her long blond hair floating behind her, her radiant blue eyes glinting in the orange light from the bonfire.

Wrapped in Bess's arms, Paul felt transported to another time and place. Away from the pep rally. Away from Wilder completely. Some place where he could have Bess to himself, for good.

He was only a sophomore in college, he knew, and Bess was only a freshman, but it felt so right already.

She's all I'll ever want—or need, he thought.

Bess pried herself out of Paul's arms and sneaked a peek over her shoulder. He followed her gaze toward Eileen. She and Emmet had finally found each other.

"They look good together, don't you think?" Bess said out loud. "Emmet's so cute." She looked at him more closely. "But why is he frowning?"

"You can thank Stephanie for that," Paul replied. "She sort of dulled his mood."

"What do you mean?"

Paul put a finger to Bess's lips. "Later. Eileen and Emmet can take care of themselves," he said, and wrapped Bess in a bear hug once again.

Bess wriggled in his arms. "But there could be trouble on the romantic front."

"There's another romantic front you seem to be forgetting about," Paul said. "And it's right here."

Cupping Bess's face in his hands, he brushed his lips against hers. Her mouth was soft and yielding, her breath warm on his face, and he kissed her deeply. This time he knew he had Bess's attention.

"I think I'm getting the message," Bess murmured, "but maybe you'd better show me again. Just to make sure . . ."

CHAPTER 3

Stephanie glanced over at Jonathan Baur sitting across the room. His gray eyes had a thoughtful look, and his attractive face was serious and concerned.

Though he hadn't said more than three words to her, Stephanie had lain awake after the rally the night before trying to think up ways to get Jonathan alone. She'd come up with ten or twelve, but none of them involved meeting him at an early Saturday morning employee meeting in the staff lounge of Berrigan's.

Will this dreary gathering *ever* end? Stephanie wondered, examining her nails.

She was slumped in the last chair in the last row in the lounge, in direct view of the clock, which read 9:35 A.M. The entire sales staff of the store was there, including Pam and another girl, Kristin St. Clair. Since Stephanie had started at Berrigan's a couple of weeks earlier, the only person she had become friendly with was Kristin, who worked in ladies' hats and accessories. Stephanie didn't know many of the other sales force. And why should she? Except for Pam and Kristin—and Jonathan, of course—everyone else was a total snore.

Stephanie crossed her long legs and picked a piece of lint off her black tights. Rubbing her eyes, she murmured to Pam: "I haven't been up this early on a Saturday morning since elementary school."

"Shh," Pam whispered, not moving her steady gaze from the man in the suit and tie standing in front of them.

"So to sum up," he was saying, "upper management is seriously concerned. Berrigan's is famous for first-rate customer service, especially its punctual, hassle-free service in ordering and shipping."

The manager paused. Stephanie, frozen in a wide yawn, realized he was glaring at her.

His tone suddenly harsher, he continued. "But this rash of late deliveries and vanishing merchandise is unacceptable. Berrigan's president, Samuel Berrigan, is afraid that if customer complaints continue at this rate, our biggest rival, J. G. Willoughby's, will take away our business. I don't need to remind you that if we lose business, some of you will lose your jobs. So stay alert, and be extra careful with all orders. If you notice anything strange, report it directly to me."

"We'd better get paid for that hour, which, by the way, was the dullest of my life," Stephanie complained to Pam and Kristin as they filed out of the room.

"I wouldn't say that too loudly if I were you," Kristin warned her. "Not if you want to keep your job."

Kristin had shoulder-length brown hair, a clean, burnished face, and big, oval, black eyes. Stephanie thought she was okay. She was tough, like her. And pretty. Also like her. And, thankfully, not too touchy-feely, like some of her suitemates. Stephanie thought she made a good-enough friend.

Stephanie scanned the small crowd. "Where is he?"

"Who?" Kristin asked.

Pam rolled her eyes. "Who else? The latest in the long list of The Men of Stephanie Keats. Hey, Steph, did you ever think of putting together your own calendar?"

"Ha, ha," Stephanie said dryly. "This is no laughing matter. Jonathan Baur is the *only* exciting thing about working in this dump. Especially since some clunk in scheduling slotted me to work the next five days in a row."

"Five? Wow, I guess that's what you get for

being low man on the totem pole. What about your exams?"

"A working girl just has to make time for everything," Stephanie said dramatically.

"Well, good luck," Kristin said good-humoredly. "I've worked here over a year, and as far as I know, Jonathan hasn't so much as had lunch with anyone female. Maybe he's married."

"No, he's not." Stephanie laughed. "He lives alone."

Pam and Kristin exchanged surprised glances. "How do you know?" they asked in unison.

Stephanie wriggled her fingers. "You just have to know who to ask. I have connections."

A cold feeling rushed up Stephanie's back as a fortyish woman with short red hair and bangs, wearing a prim navy suit, stopped in front of them.

"Hi, Alice," Pam said gently, touching her arm. "How's it going down there?"

Alice Woodward was the manager of ordering and shipping. Most of that morning's meeting had been spent criticizing her and her crew.

"As well as can be expected," Alice replied with a sorrowful shrug. "I still can't figure out all these errors. I've been checking everything twice, even three times. Anyway, sorry to be the reason you got dragged here early."

"It's no big deal," Kristin answered.

"Speak for yourself," Stephanie grumbled under her breath.

Alice shot her a cold stare. "I'll see you all later," she said to the others, then began to walk away.

"Nice," Kristin commented.

"Well, why should I be nice?" Stephanie asked. "She's had it in for me ever since I got here. So I had a little problem forgetting to initial orders in shipping, so what? I got tired of her nagging me all the time. But who wouldn't? And *she* has the gall to say I have an *attitude* problem!"

"Why, I have no idea what she means," Pam said with round eyes.

"Salespeople are supposed to initial every order that goes out," Kristin pointed out, "so if there's a problem, shipping knows who to call."

Stephanie waved Kristin's explanation away. "Whatever. Then Alice actually reports me to personnel for smoking! Can you believe that?"

"It is a no-smoking store," Pam said gingerly.

Stephanie, hands on hips, glared at her. "I was smoking on the loading dock," she explained. "Every single driver smokes out there. I don't see her turning them in. And to make it worse, I'm still in this stupid probationary period for new employees, so personnel told me if I'm caught smoking again, they might actually fire me! Have you ever heard of such drivel?"

Pam winced. "To tell you the truth, Steph—"

But Stephanie wouldn't hear it. Working in this crummy place was bad enough. Being subjected to infantile rules was downright humiliating. But having to put up with Miss Dullsville herself, too?

"No way," Stephanie seethed. "Alice Woodward has it in for me. And if her department is in a shambles, that's her fault, not mine," she said loudly.

"Keep it down," Kristin whispered out of the side of her mouth. She nodded down the hall.

Stephanie looked up. Alice Woodward was heading straight for them.

"Frankly, I'm relieved to hear you think I brought all this on myself," she said, her blue eyes staring Stephanie down. "Because then you'll understand the next time I have you reprimanded for forgetting to initial another order. Be careful, Stephanie, or you'll bring instant unemployment on yourself."

Stephanie blinked. Biting the inside of her cheek, she could feel her face flush. "Sure, sure," she said weakly.

The fact was, as wrathful as she felt toward Alice Woodward, she needed this job. Not only had her father cut off her credit cards, but there was going to be a new financial rearrangement with him. From now on she'd have to make the most of her own spending money.

As Alice strode away, Pam threw Stephanie an accusing look.

"Just don't say I told you so," Stephanie insisted.

Kristin looked at her watch. "Ten o'clock, time to take battle stations. Have a better day, Steph."

As Kristin and Pam headed in opposite directions, Stephanie headed in a third. She'd spotted the back of Jonathan Baur's head halfway down a different aisle.

So far, Stephanie's attempts to get him to notice her had not been too successful. Inconceivably, he seemed more interested in the pyramid displays of dishware and color TVs than a ravishing woman like her. But Stephanie was anything but a quitter.

Recognizing a valuable target for her affections when she saw one, she ducked low and sped down a parallel lane. Pretending to straighten up a display of food processors, she casually backed into him.

"Oops!" She smiled coyly.

Jonathan acted surprised. "Aren't you in cosmetics, Stephanie?"

Stephanie shrugged. "I was just walking by here and noticed that this display needed tidying. With everything so tense around here, I wouldn't want anyone to get into trouble."

Jonathan cocked his head. "That's very nice of you."

"We employees have to stick together," she said breezily.

Jonathan's curvy lips twisted in a slow smile. A light came to his sultry eyes that made Stephanie swallow. She noticed how stylishly he was dressed, in brown wool pants and a black merino wool cardigan.

Definitely the sign of a sensitive and mature man, she mused. But he sure doesn't talk much.

"So speaking of camaraderie," Stephanie continued, trying hard to sound casual, "I was wondering if you wanted to have lunch later."

Jonathan's eyes widened. "With you?"

"Unless you have something better planned?"

Jonathan seemed taken aback. "I usually eat alone."

"Do managers *have* to eat alone?" Stephanie asked guilelessly.

Jonathan shrugged. "Okay," he said simply. "See you at noon."

You lucky boy, Stephanie thought as she watched him walk away.

Though he hadn't exactly fallen all over himself at the invitation, she thought.

Glowing with triumph, Stephanie headed for cosmetics.

Nancy's slippered feet were kicked up on her bed, her head propped up with pillows. With a carton of orange juice on her desk beside her, she was surveying the list she'd made in her notebook.

"Kara," she called out across the room to her roommate, Kara Verbeck, who was motionless in her bed. "Tell me if I've left anything out: phone Jake's friends, put in the call for the cake, buy present, make ingenious plan to keep surprise party a secret. Well, what do you think?"

Kara emitted a barely audible grunt.

"Really?" Nancy stared uncertainly at her list. "I can't help feeling that I've left something out."

Kara's head, a faceless sun-streaked tangle, lifted up off her pillow.

"How about 'It's early Saturday morning and you just woke me from the deepest of sleeps'?" she said groggily. "Or maybe the fact that you know Jake hates surprise parties. Your choice."

Nancy sighed. "Am I the only one psyched for throwing him this party?"

"No," came Kara's reply. "But exams are just days away, you know."

Nancy sipped her juice. "Believe me, I know."

The phone started to ring, and Nancy grabbed it. "Hello?"

"Good morning!" It was Jake.

"I was just thinking about you," Nancy said.

"You mean you actually stopped?"

Nancy grinned. "Not really."

"How about a quick cup of coffee before I hole up in the library all day?"

Nancy swallowed, knowing she had to tell Jake what could be the first of many lies she'd have to invent if she was going to pull off his surprise party.

"I can't," she moaned, a little too loudly, she thought.

"Studying all day, too?" Jake said.

"Yeah, you should see me now, penned in by piles of books on all sides."

"What about tonight, then?" Jake suggested. "We could meet for a bite at the Cave."

During exams, the Cave, an artsy snacketeria below Wilder's architecture studios, became a major hangout for people on study breaks.

"Excellent" was halfway out of Nancy's mouth when she stopped herself. The truth was, she'd have liked nothing better than to hang out with Jake. But she was about to meet Bess and George for coffee to plan the party. After that she was going to be busy calling people to invite them. And running errands and ordering things for the party. Then there was the little matter of flunking her exams if she didn't study. She probably wouldn't be able to crack a book until late. She'd need the time after dinner for serious studying alone.

"I can't," she said mournfully, ransacking her brain for an excuse. After stumbling for a second, the best she could do was, "I have a study group with some people from my Western Civ class."

"On Saturday night?" Jake quizzed her. "Maybe I can help. I took that class freshman year."

"I don't think so," Nancy said uncertainly. "But thanks anyway."

"So you're blowing me off," Jake said.

Nancy laughed uneasily. "I'm sorry."

"Okay, don't worry about it," Jake said.

"You'd just better ace those exams, or I'll never forgive you."

As Nancy put down the phone, she glanced back and forth between her party list and her stack of unread notebooks. "This better be worth it."

Now she had less than five minutes to meet Bess and George at Java Joe's. Hopping out of bed, she stepped into her jeans, yanked on a sweatshirt, and grabbed her jacket. But as she reached the door, the phone started to ring again.

"Kara, will you get that?" Nancy asked. But Kara's head had vanished into her blankets.

Maybe it's Jake again, Nancy thought. "Hello?" she said breathlessly.

"Nancy?" asked the small voice on the other end.

"Anna!" Nancy said, surprised.

Anna Pedersen was Nancy's little sister in Helping Hands, a Big Brother/Big Sister program at Wilder. She was twelve and lived with her father on the other side of town. Anna and Nancy had been to movies, dinners, and shopping together, becoming close as they got to know each other.

"I'm just calling to make sure we're still getting together tomorrow," Anna said.

"Wow, I'm glad you called," Nancy replied. The fact was, as busy as she was, she'd actually forgotten all about Anna. "Hey, would you mind if we postponed? You have no idea how crazy things are right now. I'm right in the middle of exams, and I'm trying to throw Jake a surprise party. And I have to get some things done for the newspaper by Sunday night."

At first Anna didn't reply, and Nancy could hear her ragged breathing on the other end.

"Oh, really?" Anna finally replied quietly.

Great, I'm disappointing *everybody* today, Nancy thought.

But there was something in Anna's voice she hadn't heard before, something fragile. Anna was upset, Nancy could feel it.

"Anna, are you okay?"

Anna hesitated. "It's nothing. I guess I'll see you next time," she said, about to hang up.

"Wait," Nancy said quickly. "Maybe I could put something off," she offered.

"Could you? I was really looking forward to seeing you," Anna said

"No problem," Nancy added firmly. "We're on. Same time, same station."

"Thanks, Nancy," Anna said, obviously relieved. "Thanks a lot. See you tomorrow."

Something's up, Nancy thought as she put down the phone.

But before it could ring again, she sprinted out the door.

Lowering herself into her desk chair, Casey plopped her cache of goods down on the floor.

Reaching into the paper grocery sack, she

pulled out one plastic bag after another. "Dried apricots, dried apple rings, orange juice, and tortilla chips."

"Fueled and ready for work," she announced, as she surveyed the pile before her.

An hour earlier, after taking out all her notes, and leaving a trail of books and papers along the length of her bed, she'd decided she needed something to propel her into study mode. So she'd headed to the Copacetic Carrot, a health food restaurant and store.

"Okay, here goes," she said, popping a dried apricot into her mouth. She reached for her notes, grabbed the enormous textbook, and stood it up in front of her.

"Hi, there." She stared at the book and her notes. "So why doesn't all your info just leap into my brain so I can be brilliant without doing a lick of work?"

Realizing she was talking to herself, Casey cast a self-conscious look toward Stephanie's side of the room. The bed was made, the closet door was closed, the small army of cosmetic and hair accessories were lined up in orderly platoons on her dresser. She listened to the rare peace and quiet.

"The working life definitely suits her," Casey commented. "Or maybe, *her* working life suits *me.*"

Suddenly the phone rang. "Saved by the bell," she said, glancing guiltily at her books. "Hello?"

"So, how's my college genius?"

"Charley!" Casey said excitedly. She could feel her pulse quicken and her heart do a little somersault. I really *do* miss you! she thought, relieved. "Oh, I've been studying for hours!"

Charley laughed his deep, throaty laugh. "No you haven't," he scolded her. "You just cracked your books five minutes ago. Wait, let me guess, you spent the morning food shopping and you just got back, so now you're stuffing your face."

Casey broke up. "How did you know?"

"I didn't," Charley said blithely. "I guessed. But do I know you, or what?"

Gripping the phone in both hands, Casey grinned from ear to ear. "Okay, smart guy, what am I doing this very second?"

"Dying to be with me," Charley said without hesitation.

"Score one," Casey said. "I can't wait until exams blow away so I can see you over break."

"In four short years, you'll be able to see me every single day," Charley added.

"Four years is not short," Casey lamented. "But you're worth the wait."

"Our life together is worth the wait," Charley corrected her.

"You love me," Casey said.

She could practically hear Charley nodding.

"I do," he said.

Casey kissed the mouthpiece of the receiver, then spent the next fifteen minutes telling Charley about Jeanne Glasseburg, the one-acts, and Eileen and Emmet.

"Okay, okay," Charley said, and laughed. "I know you're trying to put off the studying, but I have to be at the soundstage in ten minutes. So I love you, I love you, I love you. 'Bye!"

Before Casey could say anything, Charley was gone, the phone line dead.

"I love you, too," she said anyway.

Putting down the receiver, she thought about the night before, and her little flirtation with Nick.

"So it didn't mean anything, after all," she said confidently. "I love Charley."

Casey hadn't so much as lifted a pen when there was a knock on the door. Casey jumped up and pulled open the door.

Eileen was standing in the doorway dressed in an oversize sweater, wool leggings, and earmuffs. "We're late," she said.

Casey eyed her. "For?"

"Kickoff!" Eileen said excitedly. "Emmet will be so disappointed if I miss it."

"So, it's still Emmet, is it?" Casey teased.

Eileen shrugged. "You never know. I have to cover my bases."

"That's the spirit," Casey replied. She threw a forlorn look at her books. "But I have to study."

Eileen rolled her eyes. "Study?" she gasped. "Come *on,* Case! It's a beautiful fall Saturday, there's a football game on—it's positively un-

American to stay indoors. Don't make me call the fun police."

Casey furrowed her brow. "Don't tempt me. It's already one o'clock and I haven't done a thing."

Eileen shrugged. "Neither have I. Neither has ninety-nine percent of the student body, for that matter," she insisted. "Just think of all those cute guys who are sitting there, waiting just for you. And the players in their tight little uniforms!"

Casey glared. "That's low. That's cheap."

But wincing and chewing on her lip, Casey saw as clear as day the bleachers populated with a hundred gorgeous guys, laughing and cheering— and looking her way.

Meanwhile, in the back of her brain, Charley's voice was still telling her how much he loved her.

And I love him, she swore to herself. So what's the harm in going to a little football game? Even if I *do* flirt a little. Everyone knows I'm going with Charley. So it's not like I'm actually *cheating* on him!

"Okay, you win," Casey said accusingly. "But if anyone asks, you made me do it. Give me sixty seconds to change, and we're outta here!"

"Really, you have a master's degree in business?" Stephanie purred.

She and Jonathan, looking lean and impossibly handsome, were sitting side by side on swivel stools at the lunch counter at Berrigan's, talking about something besides sales receipts.

Well, sort of. He hadn't revealed anything personal yet. In fact, Stephanie had done practically all the talking.

She raised a slender shoulder. "And you're working at Berrigan's to . . . ?" She waved a hand, urging him on.

"Gain managerial experience," Jonathan answered. "I want to open my own business one day."

Blinking with interest, Stephanie leaned in so close that it would have been hard for a passerby to see that they weren't arm in arm. "And what kind of business?"

She wanted to hear something like: bond-fund trader or import-export of exotic crafts from Africa. Something exciting, high-powered, maybe risky.

But Jonathan only shrugged. "Definitely retail."

"Retail?" Stephanie sniffed, disappointed. Then an idea materialized in her brain. "Like fashion? Or an art gallery in New York? Better yet, Paris!" She eyed him apprehensively. "Right?"

Jonathan smiled serenely and shook his head. "No, just a business here in Weston," he said.

"Oh," Stephanie said, not moving a muscle on her face. She could feel something inside her deflate, like a pricked balloon.

He may be lean and unspeakably handsome—
but not as sophisticated as I'd like. On the other
hand he is still gorgeous, she thought to herself.
Not to mention older than those immature campus dolts. And there's something about him I
can't resist, something I can't put my finger on,
though I'd like to.

"That was good," Jonathan said, folding his
napkin and placing it on the counter.

"Yes," Stephanie said dryly. "Thanks, this
was great."

Jonathan cleared his throat. "Do you want to
have lunch again tomorrow?" he asked.

Stephanie nodded. "Sure. But my treat, okay?"

Jonathan smiled and nodded, then stood up to
leave. She swiveled off her stool, and they walked
back into the store.

"I'm going to step out for some air before I
have to get back," Stephanie said. Jonathan gave
her a nod and was off to the elevator. As she
strode through electronics, Stephanie felt in her
purse for her cigarettes.

Why am I so attracted to him? she asked herself, surprised. He's kind of sweet, though sweet
is normally so *dull.* So why doesn't he seem
that way?

Pent up with tension, she headed straight for
the loading dock. "Alice Woodward or no Alice
Woodward," she muttered, "I need a smoke."

CHAPTER 4

Java Joe's was so empty and quiet that Nancy heard Bess's and George's voices the second she walked through the door.

"Hi," she said as she slid into their usual corner booth. "Where is everybody? I've never seen it so dead in here at lunchtime on a Saturday."

"Everyone's probably studying, so the afternoon will be free for the football game," said Bess.

"I'll have to head over to the library and crack the books myself sometime today," added George.

Where I should be, Nancy thought. "Sorry I'm late. Jake called just as I was leaving. He wanted to meet for lunch."

"Well, he can't have everything," George

44

quipped. "If he wants a surprise party he just has to make some sacrifices."

Bess started laughing, but Nancy was too over-whelmed by her mountain of tasks to join in. "I hope he'll want the party," she said reflectively.

"Think of it this way," George added with a casual shrug. "By the time he gets to choose, it'll be too late. Once the party train leaves the station, you know, you can't get off."

"You don't think he suspects, do you?" Nancy asked.

Bess and George exchanged mock impatient frowns.

"Okay, okay," Nancy apologized. "Let's forget about little me and my problems for a second. I need a coffee big time."

"Ditto," Bess and George replied in unison.

Nancy went to the counter and returned with three fresh caffe lattes. "So," she said, settling back into the booth, "still psyched about that act-ing class, Bess?"

Bess nodded enthusiastically. "But I have to get in first."

"We were just talking about that," George jumped in. "Our friend Bess here thinks she doesn't have a prayer."

Nancy raised an eyebrow. "Do I detect a crisis in self-confidence?"

Bess nodded mournfully. "By working with Jeanne Glasseburg," she said excitedly, "I'd learn an incredible amount. Casey said Glasseburg's one of the best acting coaches around. And she'd be an *amazing* connection. I'd do anything to get in."

Nancy was nodding thoughtfully. It was fantastic how far Bess had come since the beginning of the semester. Maybe among the three of them, she was the one who had grown the most. And if Bess was a flower, Paul Cody and her acting were the elements making her bloom.

"I hope you get into the class," Nancy said affectionately to her friend. "In fact, I'm sure you will."

"Yeah, right," Bess rolled her eyes.

"So, are you still bringing Jake home to meet your dad during the break?" George asked Nancy.

Nancy nodded. "I can't wait for exams to be over."

"Well," George continued, "then maybe we can all get together. I asked Will to come home with me."

Nancy's eyes widened. "That's great, George! That'll be so much fun! So he's going to meet your parents."

"Yep," George said. "But I'm worried. What if they don't like him?"

Bess shoved George playfully. "Fat chance. Will is so impressive, your mother will swoon."

"What about you, Bess?" Nancy asked. "Paul coming with you?"

Bess shook her head. "Not this time. He's going home to see his folks."

Nancy brought out her party list. "Vacation. Boy, it seems like years away. There's so much to do between now and then." She closed her eyes. "When am I going to study for my exams? Plus I promised Anna I'd see her tomorrow."

Bess touched her hand. "Your life does seem a little crazy right now."

Nancy gave her a brief, humorless smile. "Thanks."

"So what can we do?" George asked.

"Yeah," Bess said, leaning forward enthusiastically. "We want to help."

Nancy smiled broadly. "I was *really* hoping you'd say that. Here." She slid a list of names across the table. "If you can call these people and tell them Wednesday eight forty-five sharp, that would be so great."

"You got it," George replied.

"And make sure they know they have to be there *on time,*" Nancy reminded them. "And they can't tell anybody. Jake hears everything. He has informants for potential stories for the paper planted all over campus—"

Nancy looked up at the clock on the wall. "I have to get going," she said abruptly. "The bakery is calling me at the *Wilder Times* office in ten minutes. They were so busy when I phoned that they had to call me back."

"But why there?" George asked.

Nancy threw up her hands. "Because on top of everything, I forgot I had two articles to proof for Monday's edition!"

Taking a last puff of her cigarette, Stephanie leaned back against a yellow forklift.

"I hate this job," she grumbled between drags.

But the chiseled face of Jonathan Baur loomed in front of her eyes like a harvest moon. If it weren't for him, she would have told Alice Woodward to stuff it days ago. Jonathan—and, well, the matter of her little debt and spending money.

After expertly flicking the cigarette butt off the loading dock, Stephanie stumbled over one of the huge prongs on the forklift. But as she straightened up, she noticed something strange: a box wedged behind one of the back wheels of the lift.

"Weird," she whispered. She peeked over her shoulder. Seeing no one, she bent down, picked up the box, and lifted the lid.

"Hmm." The box was stuffed with half a dozen sweaters. "Straight off the rack," Stephanie said to herself. "The tags are still on them . . . oh, and not *inexpensive* sweaters either."

There were vests and cardigans and pullovers, all lambswool, Berrigan's finest.

That's so weird, she thought. Why would someone leave a box of brand-new sweaters under the forklift wheel?

Suddenly Stephanie froze. "Oh no!" She

looked at her watch. I'm ten minutes late. That's just what Mrs. Caldwell is waiting for. And Alice! I'm history!

Stephanie raced inside, then slowed to a walk on her tiptoes as she came to a doorway marked Ordering and Shipping Dept., Alice Woodward, Mgr. Peeking inside and seeing that the coast was clear, Stephanie hopped across the narrow doorway and ran for the employee locker room, just off the lounge.

She walked the row of lockers until she came to hers, then stared blankly. Numbers had never been her forte, especially combination locks.

She turned the knob right, left, "Thirty-two . . . twenty-five . . . ten . . . !" But the handle wouldn't budge.

She looked at her watch. Twelve minutes late. Pam was going to kill her. She couldn't take her break until Stephanie came back.

"And one more thing," came an angry voice from the lounge. It was Alice! "I still don't see how we could have screwed up this order, too, if you did everything you said you did."

Another mess up, Stephanie realized. Poor Alice, she thought. But poor Alice wouldn't appreciate the pack of cigarettes and lighter in Stephanie's hand. Quickly Stephanie turned back to her locker. "Thirty-two . . . twenty-five . . . *twenty* . . . there, got it!"

Stephanie tossed her cigarettes inside, then realized she still had the box of sweaters under her arm. She shrugged. A potential present for Alice? "She'd be so pleased," Stephanie thought out loud. "Just another of someone else's screwups."

"Look, mister, this isn't funny," Alice's voice rang out down the hall. "This is your job on the line!"

Hmm, Stephanie thought. Maybe this isn't the best of times to give Alice a gift. Maybe I should just put the box back where I found it—

"Stephanie!"

Stephanie cringed. But turning, she breathed a sigh of relief. "Oh, it's only you."

"Yeah, only me," Pam said angrily, her hands on her hips. "I've been looking for you everywhere, Stephanie! Where have you been?"

"Right here?" Stephanie replied meekly.

Pam crossed her arms. "You have bad timing. The manager's really ticked off, especially after the meeting this morning. I had to make yet another excuse on your behalf, but I don't think he's buying it. And I'm starving. My lunch break should have started fifteen minutes ago."

"Sorry, I'm on my way," Stephanie said hurriedly, then stared at the box in her hands. No time to give this to Alice, no time to explain it to Pam, no time *period.*

Tossing the box into her locker, Stephanie slammed the door, spun the lock, and breezed past Pam toward the stairs.

"Sorry again, Pam," she tossed back over her shoulder. "Enjoy your lunch."

Nancy's face was flushed with excitement as she marched along the pathway that crisscrossed the main quad, toward the *Wilder Times* offices.

In the distance, she could hear the roar from Holliston Stadium. The campus clock tower said one o'clock, and Nancy figured that the game had just gotten under way. It was a clear, crisp afternoon; the leaves were skittering across the lawn, the clouds racing one another across the sky. Perfect weather for football. She took the steps up to the second floor of the media arts building.

Usually the *Times* office was alive with office sounds: clicking keyboards, ringing telephones, shouting people. But like Java Joe's, the office was deserted and quiet. The computer monitors were blank and the cubicles looked empty.

"All the better," Nancy said to herself. With Jake safely at the Rock, she could use the office phone to finish the calls for the party.

Setting her book bag down on her desk, Nancy was about to lower herself into her chair when the phone rang. But before she could reach it, the ringing stopped.

"Hello, *Times*," a deep voice said from a cubicle across the room. A deep, *familiar* voice.

"Jake?" Nancy called. She peeked over the top of her partition. Across the room, Jake's black cowboy boots were crossed at the ankles on top of his desk, his thermal mug steaming with coffee.

"What are you doing here?" she asked.

Jake smiled up at her, holding up his hand for quiet. "Who's calling? Mario's? For *whom?*"

The bakery! Nancy realized. She sprinted across the office and snatched the phone out of Jake's hand.

"Hi!" she said in a falsely bright voice. "You can do the interview? Great!"

Her heart galloping, Nancy cast a sidelong glance at Jake to see what he'd picked up. The baker on the other end, she realized, didn't know what she was talking about.

"Interview?" the baker was saying. "I'm calling about a cake. I'm looking for a Nancy Drew."

Smiling through her nervousness, Nancy nodded. "Uh-huh, that's right."

"Look, I don't know what's going on," the baker said irritably, "but if you want this cake you need to drop off a deposit before I start working on it."

"I understand," Nancy replied. "I'll do that. I'll meet you there."

"Who's Mario?" Jake asked when she put down the phone.

Nancy waved. "Just an interview for a story. Hey," she said quickly, trying to divert him, "what are you doing here?"

"I just came by to drop off the rewrite for Monday's lead," Jake explained.

"And you didn't hear me come in?"

"You know me." Jake laughed. "I got distracted by next week's story, and one thing led to another. I was concentrating—" He eyed her, puzzled. "And why shouldn't I be here, anyway?"

"What happened to the Rock?"

"It's still there." Jake cocked his head. "So now you're studying all day *and* doing an interview?"

Nancy quickly put on an aloof expression that wouldn't have convinced even her. "It's just a story I'm tracking."

"During exam week? Why didn't you tell me about it?" Jake asked.

Nancy was trapped.

I'm a terrible liar! she chided herself.

Then she thought of a way out: pick a small fight, confuse him.

"Do you have to know about everything I do?" she said in her best annoyed tone of voice. "What's the big deal? I've got a lot to do right now, okay?"

Arching his eyebrows, Jake slapped his thighs and stood. "Okay," he said. "I can see we're a little stressed at the moment. I'd better be getting back to the Rock anyway. Have your secretary give me a call when you can squeeze me into your busy schedule."

"Hey you!" Nancy called after him as he began to walk out.

Jake turned and waited for a few seconds, but

Nancy realized that she couldn't explain without giving everything away. She took his hands and gave them a squeeze. "I hope your studying goes well," she said lamely. "I'm sorry if I snapped at you."

"Me, too," he replied, giving her hands a squeeze back. He gave her a crooked smile, more puzzled than happy, then abruptly let go of her and pushed through the door.

"He knows something's up," Nancy murmured disconsolately to herself.

"What interview *were* you talking about?"

At the sound of the voice, Nancy whirled around. Gail Gardeski, the paper's editor-in-chief, was standing in the doorway to her office, her arms crossed, a small, knowing smile on her face.

Gail was pretty in a hard, thin way. Her piercing eyes were magnified behind small round glasses.

"You heard all that?" Nancy asked, blushing with embarrassment.

Gail nodded. "It was kind of hard to miss. You guys seemed to be talking past each other."

Nancy lowered herself into her chair. "We were. Literally. On top of studying and doing those proofs I promised you, I'm trying to plan a huge surprise party for Jake to celebrate the *Chicago Herald*'s running his piece."

Gail gave her a big nod. "I get it. And Mario?"

"The baker," Nancy replied. "For a congratulations cake."

Gail started to laugh.

"You didn't buy the interview thing?" Nancy asked.

Gail shook her head. "Sorry, but no. And by the way, Jake's only the best investigative reporter at Wilder. Good luck trying to keep *this* a secret from him."

Nancy hid her face in her hands. "What a disaster. Well, anyway, you're invited to the party. It's Wednesday night, eight forty-five, at Jake's apartment. Though, at this rate, I doubt Jake will be there."

"Think of it this way," Gail said. "At least you'll have a great cake."

As the game ended, Emmet trotted to the sidelines and peered up into the packed bleachers. All the players on the Wilder sideline were slapping high fives. Everyone in the crowd was clapping and screaming. Emmet held up the game ball and pumped it in the air. The fans exploded.

A ball was given every game to the most valuable player. And there was no doubt that that day's star was Emmet Lehman.

With the Norsemen down by three points in the last minute, Emmet had taken a handoff and streaked sixty yards for the game-winning touchdown, beating their arch-rivals Coldwater State and ensuring Wilder's perfect record in the conference.

"Hey, awesome run!" his teammates were yelling to him, slapping his shoulder pads.

Emmet was delirious with joy, not only because all his friends were in the stands, but also because one fan in particular had seen him.

"Emmet!"

Emmet whirled. But all he saw was chaos: people smiling in his face, pumping his hand.

"Emmet, over here!"

Emmet shouldered his way through his teammates and saw Eileen snaking down the aisle toward the field with Casey trailing behind her.

Gripping his ball tighter, Emmet could feel the rush through to his fingertips. Of course he was elated about the game, but right now he was totally psyched that Eileen had seen it.

"That was amazing!" Eileen cried when she reached the bottom.

"Pretty impressive, Lehman," Casey added. "You looked like a track star. That run at the end made blowing off all my work really worth it."

Eileen tried to give him a congratulatory hug, but couldn't get her arms around the shoulder pads. "I didn't know you were such a star."

Emmet could feel his face heat up through the sweat. "Thanks," he said modestly. "I'm really glad you were here."

"I wouldn't have missed it!" Eileen replied.

"Even after last night? I thought I might have been kind of a dud."

"Well, Stephanie doesn't exactly inspire us all to laughter and good times," Casey joked.

Emmet noticed that Casey's eyes were roaming over his teammates, checking them out.

"Hey, I want to give you something," Emmet said to Eileen quietly.

"Me?" Eileen looked astonished. "I feel like I should give *you* something. You won the game all by yourself."

"It wasn't by myself, but thanks, anyway," he said. "Here, I want you to have this."

Emmet gently took Eileen's hand, pried open her gloved fingers, and rested the game ball in her palm. Grass and dirt were caught in the laces, but it was the ball he'd carried into the end zone.

Eileen stared at him, her mouth agape. "Really? You want me to have this?"

Emmet nodded. "So I know we'll go out again sometime. And I'll know where it is."

This time it was Eileen's turn to blush. "That's sweet," she said. "I don't know what to say."

"Say thanks."

"Hey, I have a better idea," she said excitedly. "I have a killer exam to study for, but I was going to take a break tomorrow afternoon to check out the opening of the new art exhibit down at the Kaplan Arts Center. It should be pretty cool. Want to come with me?"

Emmet tried but failed to drum up any enthusiasm. The day after a game he was always really sore, and during that day's game he'd run more than usual. Besides, art didn't exactly excite him. In fact, he knew next to nothing about it.

But so what? he thought to himself. He'd be out with Eileen, and she was an art major. It would probably mean a lot to her.

"Sure," he said eagerly. "Why not?"

"Great, I'll call you tomorrow," Eileen replied. "Oh, and Emmet? I'm really proud of you."

As he watched Eileen drag Casey away, Emmet never felt so calm. Finally, a breakthrough. First through the line of scrimmage. And now through the wall around Eileen's heart.

CHAPTER 5

"Boy, standing around on your feet all day isn't easy," Pam said as she headed for the stairs. The six o'clock closing signal had just sounded through Berrigan's. All over the store, the employees were ringing out, straightening up shelves, and heading for the locker room.

"You're not kidding," Stephanie repeated dubiously as she limped behind. "My feet are killing me. I can't even feel my right big toe."

"That's why they tell you not to wear three-inch heels."

"Well," Stephanie said, "you have to make an impression. And my face is numb from flashing all those fake smiles."

"Maybe you need more practice," Pam joked. "Smiling is one of those things that usually comes naturally to people."

Stephanie snorted. "Speak for yourself. Anyway, I'm glad to see you're not mad at me any more for blowing your lunch hour."

"I don't get mad," Pam said with a wink, "I get even."

Down in the employee lounge, it seemed as if the entire sales staff was milling around, talking at once. Alice Woodward was standing off to one side, looking even more unhappy than she had that morning.

Stephanie could see why. Upper management was back. Alice, it seemed, was on the wrong end of a lecture.

"What now?" Stephanie asked.

Jonathan stepped forward. "Yesterday, an order was shipped to Berrigan's biggest client, but when it arrived, it was short six items."

"I swear there were the correct number of boxes," Alice Woodward said defensively. "I've been counting all the orders myself before Eagle Express comes to pick up."

"And you're sure you counted the sweaters?" the manager challenged her.

For the first time, Alice seemed totally defeated. "I'm sure," she insisted weakly.

Pam walked over and laid a sympathetic hand on her shoulder. "You'll figure it out, Alice."

"I just hope it's before I lose my job," Alice replied.

"What did you say the missing items were?" Stephanie interrupted.

Alice looked up and narrowed her eyes. "Why would you care?"

Stephanie pictured the box she found behind the forklift that afternoon. "Just curious."

"Sweaters," the manager informed her. "Six lambswool sweaters."

"How interesting."

Nonchalantly, Stephanie crossed the room toward her locker while conversation continued behind her. Calmly, but making certain to keep her cigarettes hidden, Stephanie fished the gift box out of her locker. Then, recrossing the room, she patiently waited for a pause in conversation before handing it over to Alice.

"Is this what you're looking for?"

For a few long seconds, Alice stared at the box. Then she opened the lid, counted the sweaters, inspected their tags, and reclosed the lid. Alice shot Stephanie an accusing glare:

"Care to explain where you got those?"

As Nancy left Mario's Bakery and headed down College Avenue, the street lamps were popping on. The streets themselves were quiet, most of the stores closing up.

It didn't really feel like a Saturday night. Zeta was the only frat having a party, to celebrate that day's victory, but everyone else seemed to have plans to study.

"Okay, so the cake's taken care of." Nancy ticked it off a mental list. "And I called everyone.

61

I have to pick up plates and streamers and stuff, but that can wait until Tuesday." Nancy breathed a sigh of relief. "Now all I have to do is meet Bess and George to iron out some details. Then I *have* to get going on that paper."

Turning the corner past Berrigan's, Nancy walked toward the department store's big double doors and spotted Stephanie, Pam, and another girl whom Nancy didn't know, standing outside.

As she got closer, Nancy noticed something was up. The three girls weren't exactly arguing, but they were having an animated discussion.

Stephanie seemed to be defending herself. "I can't believe she doesn't believe me."

"I can," Pam replied coolly.

"Pam!" Stephanie almost shrieked. She waved her hands in frustration and disbelief.

The third girl stepped between them. "Chill, you guys."

"Hey, what's up?" Nancy said.

Pam smiled weakly. "Hi, Nance."

"Nothing," Stephanie snapped.

Nancy raised an eyebrow. "Really? Just another average day at Berrigan's?"

"Anything but," Pam replied. "Do you know Kristin?"

Nancy offered her hand. "Hi. I'm Nancy."

Kristin smiled. Nancy thought she was pretty, with very short, brown, curly hair and an open, good-natured face. "We're just having a little problem," she started to explain.

"It may be a problem," Stephanie cut in, "but it's not mine."

"It is now," Pam retorted. "At least that's what Alice says."

Stephanie leveled a blazing glare at her. "Why are you always protecting Alice? The woman has it in for me. Not to mention the fact that she is one hundred percent, completely wrong about this."

Nancy noticed that all three of them were focused on her, as if she had the answer. "Don't look at me," she said with a laugh. "I have no idea what you're talking about."

"There's been an epidemic of mistakes in ordering and shipping," Pam explained. "Like missing stuff, merchandise vanishing, or a bunch of little screwups such as people forgetting to initial orders."

"Yeah, and supposedly they're all my fault," Stephanie added. "And if it rains, that'll be my fault, too. Like today," she went on, and told Nancy the story of finding the sweaters and Alice's accusing her of taking them.

"You may have found them on the loading dock," Nancy said after hearing Stephanie out, "but you have to admit, Steph, it would look kind of suspicious to Alice."

Pam, arms crossed, was nodding.

"You think Steph's lying?" Nancy asked Pam, surprised. Stephanie wasn't exactly the most open and virtuous person on campus, but Nancy never thought of her as a liar, not to mention a thief.

"I don't think Stephanie was trying to steal the sweaters, if that's what you mean," Pam answered.

"Thanks for your vote of confidence." Stephanie sniffed.

"But something's definitely screwy," Pam went on, "and I'm sorry, Steph, but I do feel sorry for Alice. She'll be fired if this stuff keeps up, and she's scared. The ironic thing is, until now she's been a model employee with a perfect record."

"Sounds like she's had a run of bad luck," Nancy surmised.

Stephanie shrugged. "It's not luck. It's just deserts. I don't feel sorry for her. Management's giving her a chance to smooth it out."

"Which is more than most stores do," Kristin said.

"What do you mean?" Pam asked.

"My father never had a chance like that. He worked at Dancor's, the big department store chain, for thirty years, and was one of their best employees. Well, he started to have some health problems. And one day he went to work when he wasn't feeling well—he was the most dedicated man in the world—and he made a mistake with some receipts that day. He was fired on the spot. It didn't matter that he'd made the mistake because he'd been sick."

"Ouch." Nancy winced.

Pam shook her head. "Harsh."

"A stab in the back is more like it," Kristin went on. "He loved Dancor's. He hasn't really been the same since."

"Hey," Nancy said, glancing at her watch. "I didn't realize how late it was. I have to get going. I hope you guys figure this out. And, Steph, don't forget. You need this job. If I were you, I'd swallow my pride and make nice to Alice. Later, guys."

As Nancy trotted down the sidewalk, she could hear Stephanie grumble, "Good thing you're not me!"

Jake was thinking about Nancy as he leaned into the chilly wind and made his way across the quad toward the Cave. It was six-thirty, and he'd been studying for five hours straight, nursing a splitting headache. He had another four good hours of studying in him if only he could get some coffee.

And if he could stop thinking about how strange Nancy had acted that afternoon. She was a knockout, she was sensitive, bitingly smart, and quick-witted—and supposedly they were in love.

"So why was she acting like such a weirdo?" he wondered aloud. "She couldn't find five minutes to take a study break with me today? And then she's making appointments to do an interview, and won't tell me anything about it? No way. Something's up."

Jake could tell the Cave was packed just by

looking in through the windows. The Cave, grungy by day, came to life at night and during exam week. One of Jake's favorite places on campus, the ceiling was a canopy of glued-together soda cans. Colorful paintings of dragons and bizarre futuristic buildings wrapped around the walls.

Inside, the atmosphere was electric. Everyone was talking about one of two things—the football game or exams.

Jake stocked up on a jumbo coffee, a brownie, and a bag of chips, and was on his way out when he spotted Bess sitting at a huge slate table. As he headed over, he saw that Paul was there, too, and George, and Bess's roommate, Leslie King. They all had their heads together, talking about something.

"Hey," Jake said.

Bess lifted her head. Her blue eyes widened with surprise. "Jake!"

Everyone at the table instantly fell silent. They all had arranged fake stiff smiles on their faces.

George nodded at Jake's loot. "Um, nutritious."

"Survival kit," Jake quipped. He noticed they were all exchanging uneasy glances. "Am I interrupting?"

"Not at all, not at all," Paul said stiffly. "We were just talking about—"

"Exams!" Leslie kicked in. "George and I were just comparing notes for calculus. All those nasty formulas. You know how it is."

Well, Leslie certainly seems chipper, Jake thought to himself.

Leslie, famous on campus for being a study grind, used to be as friendly and sensitive as a drill sergeant. A premed major from birth, she'd demanded perfect silence during designated study hours at night. Lately, though, she'd had a change of heart, had become less uptight about everything. In fact, she'd started to become a pleasant, normal human being. She was even happily involved with some guy named Nathan.

"Well, don't let me interrupt," Jake said. "I was just heading back to the Rock. You haven't seen Nancy by any chance, have you?"

"Right behind you," Leslie said.

Jake reeled around. "Nancy!"

The second he saw her, his uneasiness from the afternoon evaporated. Nancy was clutching her books to her chest, her glistening strawberry blond hair hanging loose around her shoulders. Her cheeks were rosy from the cold. Jake felt like hugging her. He would have done anything to get her alone, even if it meant blowing off the rest of his studying.

But Nancy obviously didn't have the same thing in mind. "What are you doing here?" she asked.

"You mean I'm not allowed to be here, either?"

Nancy seemed unsure of what to say. "Of course you're allowed," she said, suddenly smiling that easy smile again.

"You look beautiful," Jake said, and grinned.

Nancy glowed at his praise. "You've been studying too hard," she said, blushing.

"So how's the big scoop going?"

"Oh . . . that," Nancy replied, her eyes wandering around the table at her friends. "As well as can be expected, I guess."

Jake felt a twinge of sadness that she wouldn't tell him what she was writing. Maybe it was a sign of independence. Maybe it was a good thing. Who knew?

"Well, keep at it," he said. "I'm sure it's going to be great." He looked down at his armful of junk food. "You want to help me lighten some of this load? We could get a table over there." He nodded toward a small round table in the corner. "I feel like I haven't seen you alone in a year."

For a second Jake thought she was going to say yes. He could see it in her eyes.

But she didn't. "Thanks, but I have that study group."

Jake stepped back from her. "Sure," he said. "I know you're busy."

Maybe she really is mad at me, he wondered. But for what?

He racked his brain for some memory of something he might have done. He was always doing goofy stuff to make her laugh. Maybe he had told one joke too many.

"Look, I'm really sorry," Jake blurted out.

Now it was Nancy's turn to give him a strange look. "What for?"

Jake shrugged. "I don't know. For whatever I did wrong."

Nancy laughed gleefully. "I don't know what you're talking about, but I love you." She grabbed the collar of his coat and kissed him hard on the mouth. "Now get back to your study carrel and be brilliant. I have work to do!"

Jake headed back out into the night, more confused than ever.

That was not the kiss of an angry woman, he told himself, biting his lower lip. She's crazy about you, Collins. You're just uptight. You're reading too much into things.

CHAPTER 6

Early the next morning Nancy arrived at Java Joe's and slid into a corner booth with a large cappuccino, a cinnamon honey bun, a stack of books, and a small mountain of index cards.

The early fall sunlight was streaming in through the nearest window, warming her face and her just-washed hair. She closed her eyes for a second, composed and relaxed and ready to face a long day of studying and seeing Anna. And of course more party planning.

"Time to crank," Nancy finally commanded herself. She opened a book, read a line, jotted a note on a card. She did it again. Then, automatically, she leaned back against the bench, fingering the ends of her hair absentmindedly.

I know what I spaced on! she suddenly

realized. What can I possibly get Jake as a present?

As the most unconventional person on the planet, Nancy knew Jake would be tough to shop for. He didn't have many possessions, but then again, he didn't need, or want, many. He was simple and focused: schoolwork, writing for the paper—and her. That was his life.

But I want to get him a congratulations gift, Nancy mused. Something he'll love.

Maybe a new pair of cowboy boots? Nancy wondered.

Forget it. He'll never give up the ones he has. He's already had the soles on those replaced three times.

Chewing nervously on the tip of her pen, Nancy scanned the little café to see if anything caught her eye.

Nothing.

All she saw were counter people in aprons and Wilder baseball caps, and a few people like her, bent over a book or a section of the Sunday paper, in uninspiring sweats.

Work! the little part of her brain reminded her.

And she did—for about three minutes, long enough to fill one notecard.

Yawning and hopelessly distracted, Nancy raised her arms over her head in a long stretch. But as she did, she froze, and squinted in disbelief. There it was, the present for Jake. It had just come through the door and was heading her way, safely clutched in someone else's hands.

It was a beautiful, pocket-size, leather-bound notebook, embossed with an intricate design on the cover. Perfect for a reporter. Easy to carry around, ideal for jotting down ideas, or taking notes during an interview.

Nancy was staring at it so hard, she didn't realize that the person holding it had stopped right in front of her.

"Nancy?"

Nancy reluctantly tore her eyes away from the notebook. "Oh, hi, Terry."

Terry Schneider was the chairman of the Focus Film Society, a campus group that screened classic movies. And in an ironic coincidence that was half-pleasant and half-eerie, he looked almost exactly like Ned Nickerson, Nancy's old boyfriend from River Heights. He and Nancy had just recently become friends, after she started attending the society's screenings.

"I see you like my notebook." Terry smiled. "I was afraid you were going to burn a hole right through it."

Nancy blinked. Whenever she saw Terry, she needed a second or two to get over his resemblance to Ned. Ned had been her closest friend, and her love for a couple of years. There was a time she thought they might actually get married. . . .

Of course he isn't really anything like Ned,

Nancy thought, shaking herself out of her reminiscing.

Finally she laughed. "I've been looking for the perfect gift for Jake, and unfortunately, it belongs to you."

Terry bent down to whisper in Nancy's ear. "I'll share a little secret with you. This isn't the only notebook like this on the planet."

"You know where I can get another one?" she asked excitedly.

"I know where you can get a thousand," Terry said. "My uncle makes them. He gave me this one last year."

Nancy grazed the smooth, beautifully crafted leather with her fingers. "And it has your initials engraved on the cover," she said. She looked up and smiled into Terry's handsome face. "The perfect gift for the man who has everything."

It's bad enough that I have to work the Sunday shift, Stephanie reflected. But then to be dragged into personnel first thing in the morning and interrogated like a prisoner of war?

She was sitting across the desk from the personnel manager, Mrs. Caldwell. Alice Woodward was sitting to her right, Ms. Glass, manager of cosmetics to her left, and Jonathan, her floor manager, was behind her, pacing the floor.

"I like you, Stephanie, or else I wouldn't have hired you," Mrs. Caldwell said. "So we just want to go over this sweater incident one more time."

Making a show of crossing her long legs, Stephanie leaned forward, pursing her ruby red lips.

"Of course," she said cooperatively. "I'd be happy to."

"Now, yesterday you said that you found the box when you were dropping an order off in the shipping department," Alice said.

Stephanie nodded. Her face was placid, her eyes focused, her hands casually clasped. But her heart was thumping.

She knew that if she'd told them she'd found the box while she was smoking out on the loading dock, that would be strike two, and Mrs. Caldwell would have had no choice but to let her go. The point was that she'd found the box. Where, was irrelevant.

"There wasn't anything shipped out of cosmetics yesterday," Ms. Glass declared.

Swallowing hard, Stephanie struggled not to show her sudden nervousness.

"So if you lied about that," Alice said pointedly, "why should we believe your story about finding the sweaters?"

Stephanie turned around and caught Jonathan's eye. "Are you actually saying I *stole* those sweaters?"

Jonathan's chiseled features were flattened by his pained expression. His hands clasped behind his back, he continued to pace, unable to meet Stephanie's gaze.

"We're not making any accusations here, Stephanie," Mrs. Caldwell insisted.

"Good, because if I did steal those sweaters," Stephanie said, "then why on earth would I have handed them over to Alice in front of fifteen witnesses? Who would be so stupid?"

Mrs. Caldwell threw up her hands. "Exactly. We're just trying to figure this thing out."

"So what about that mysterious order to ship?" Alice wanted to know.

Stephanie cleared her throat and raised her chin indignantly. "Okay, I found them behind the forklift," she admitted. "So what?"

"The forklift on the loading dock?" Alice asked calmly.

Mrs. Caldwell acted confused. "Why didn't you say that in the first place?"

"Because she was smoking—*again*," Alice insinuated with a stern nod.

"I was not!" Stephanie protested quickly. "I had lunch with Jonathan, and it had been stuffy in the restaurant, so I needed some fresh air before I went back to cosmetics."

"She was smoking," Alice muttered conclusively.

"Prove it," Stephanie replied haughtily. "I promised I wouldn't smoke, and I keep my promises," she declared, almost choking on her bald-faced lie. "Besides, are we trying to track down this little problem you're having, Alice, or do we want to spend all day talking about some dumb cigarettes?"

Stephanie felt a stab of triumph as Alice sat there in frustrated silence.

Mrs. Caldwell looked at Alice. "Anything else?"

But Alice just shook her head.

"Maybe you should be talking to Pam," Stephanie tossed out. "After all, I saw her downstairs near the shipping office yesterday."

"Pam Miller would never do anything like this!" Alice objected.

"We're not jumping to conclusions here," Mrs. Caldwell said. "Now, Alice, this is still your department's responsibility. Ms. Keats should be allowed to get back to work. All I can say is double your efforts."

Alice rose from her chair and, without even glancing at Stephanie, stalked out in cold silence.

As the meeting broke up, Stephanie approached Jonathan. All the hardness melted from her face.

"I wish I could help clear all this up, Jonathan." Stephanie looked at him nervously. "Are we still on for lunch today?"

Jonathan was still acting troubled. "All right," he said. He stared at her a moment. "Be careful, Stephanie, okay?" His tone was soft, but the warning was unmistakable.

Does he think I did it, too? she wondered as she slowly wandered back to cosmetics.

That was one thing about Jonathan that bothered her—and intrigued her—she realized. As much as she couldn't take her eyes off him, she still couldn't get inside. Who was Jonathan Baur? Was he shy and quiet? Or was he sharp, careful, and pensive? Jonathan Baur looked like the man of her dreams, but was he?

Emmet grimaced as he and Eileen walked up the path to the Kaplan Center of the Arts.

"Still sore?" Eileen asked.

"It's nothing." Emmet smiled.

The truth was, he'd pulled a muscle in his leg, both his knees were throbbing, his neck was stiff, and he had a large welt over his left eye. In fact, Sundays he usually reserved for napping and eating and soaking his body in the whirlpool. And maybe a little studying, if he had the energy.

"Isn't this building cool?" Eileen asked, gazing up. "My suitemate Liz, who's an architecture student, told me it's a Pope."

"A what?" Emmet asked.

"Frederick Pope? The architect?"

"Right," Emmet said, nodding as if he recognized the name, even though it meant nothing to him.

He had to lean far back to see the top of the building without moving his neck. The Kaplan Center was a giant, ultramodern cube made out of poured concrete and glass. Now he knew this Pope guy designed it, which he guessed was a big deal. But Emmet liked the older buildings on campus better, the ones with columns and ivy crawling up the brick walls. They seemed homey and friendly, while the Kaplan Arts Center seemed cold and intimidating. Especially since it housed Wilder's art museum and the fine arts department, which Emmet knew nothing about.

"Let's go in," Eileen said excitedly. To Emmet's surprise, she gave his hand a quick squeeze.

"Wow!" Eileen said as they entered the gallery.

Emmet looked up, interested and open-minded. But as Eileen stepped up to a huge painting and inspected it carefully, Emmet hung back and cocked his head. The canvas was set in a beautiful wooden frame and was titled *Weather*.

But however he looked at it, right side up or sideways, to Emmet it looked like someone had taken a house-painting brush and slapped around three or four colors of house paint.

He moved on to the next one. He thought he could identify a human shape, but it was twisted, and he didn't think it was drawn all that well. The arms and legs were really huge. It was called, *Untitled No. 54.*

Emmet wandered over to a table in the middle of the gallery that had cheese and crackers and soda. He helped himself and let his eyes roam over the walls, trying to pick out something he liked so he'd have something positive to say later.

There were two or three paintings that he liked. They were beautiful landscapes, set in the country, which reminded Emmet of the farm he grew up near.

"Well, what do you think?" Eileen asked, coming up to him.

Emmet hadn't been able to come up with much to say. "I like those landscapes. What do you think?"

Eileen squinted, nodding thoughtfully. She pointed toward the corner, at a painting of blue and red *X*'s and *O*'s. "I really like the way that person was using paint," she said.

To do what? Emmet wondered to himself. It just looked like blobs of color. He didn't see the point. Just then a blond girl came walking over.

"Hi, Holly!" Eileen greeted her. "This is Emmet."

Emmet shook the hand of a tall, gracefully pretty woman, who smiled pleasantly at him.

"Holly's in my sorority," Eileen explained. "Actually, a lot of the people here are Kappas. I think we have more art majors than any other sorority on campus."

Holly was nodding proudly, looking at Emmet expectantly. But what could he say? From what he could see, he didn't think much of Wilder's art majors.

Emmet thought Eileen seemed disappointed that he wasn't saying anything. "Emmet's the football hero from yesterday," she told Holly.

"Oh," Holly said. "Who won?"

Eileen smiled. "We did!" she said. "Emmet did it all by himself. Tell me you didn't hear?"

Holly shook her head. "Sorry, I didn't. Congratulations."

"It's okay, not everybody's into football," Emmet said quietly. "Thanks."

"So what do you think of the exhibit?" Holly asked.

Emmet's smile froze on his lips.

Suddenly someone brushed against him, a tall, slender guy in a black turtleneck and black jeans. His hair was slicked back in a ponytail. He was standing next to a woman who was wearing bloodred lipstick and little round glasses. They were looking at the big painting called *Weather*.

"What this painting is after," the guy was saying, "is a kind of approximation of our inner thoughts, intersected by the weather outside, forming a kind of discourse of internal and external circumstance. The lack of recognizable form is important, because we never know what we're thinking anyway."

Emmet threw Eileen and Holly a sidelong glance. But they'd turned to listen and were concentrating on what the guy was saying.

"Excuse me," Emmet said to Eileen and Holly, unable to hold himself back, "but what is he talking about?"

Eileen cocked his head. "What do you mean, what is he talking about?"

Emmet had a feeling that he'd made a big mistake opening his mouth. But he didn't care. He wasn't stupid. He had a right to an opinion, too.

"What I mean is," he said, "I have no clue what that guy was saying. What's the point of art if you can't tell what it is? To me a painting should tell a story, or have some *thing* in it that you can recognize without a long explanation. My dog could do better than that painting."

The second Emmet finished talking, he knew he was right about making a mistake. But it was too late. Emmet noticed the man and woman had overheard him. The guy whipped around, his face flushed with anger.

"What do *you* know about art?" he asked arrogantly. "Do you know how long that painting took to execute?"

Emmet glanced at the painting, then said, simply, "It looks like it took five minutes."

"Five minutes!" the guy sputtered. "How dare you spew such ignorance about my work!"

Blushing, Emmet pointed. "That's *yours?*"

As the dread worked its way up from his stomach, Emmet's mouth became dry.

The artist and his friend stalked away.

"I didn't know it was his work. I'm sorry if I insulted the guy," Emmet started to explain. "Even if his painting looks like the collective work of a kindergarten class."

Holly looked shocked. "Kindergarten!"

As Emmet saw the expression on Eileen's face

change from surprise to anger, he wanted to crawl under a rock.

Not only did I insult Eileen's taste in art, Emmet lamented, now I've offended her friends. Maybe *her* paintings look like these. There's no way this relationship has a chance!

CHAPTER 7

Nancy knew something wasn't right the second Anna slid into the passenger seat of her Mustang. During the drive into downtown Weston, Anna answered Nancy's questions with little more than a shrug. School was "okay." Her dad was "okay." Life in general was "okay." Her long blond hair was messy and draped like a curtain in front of her face.

Not exactly the Anna Nancy had met a few weeks ago. Before she got involved with Helping Hands, Nancy knew that most of the kids who entered the program needed attention. Anna's mother had died three years earlier, when Anna was nine, and her father was usually at his job until late in the evening. Anna had definitely been a candidate for an older friend like Nancy.

Anna turned out to be sweet and lively, with a canny sense of humor that was beyond her years.

Not today, though. During lunch, Anna hardly touched her food or lifted her soft brown eyes from her plate.

"Hey," Nancy said cheerfully as they left Anthony's, a sandwich place downtown, "you want to cruise by the arcade?"

Anna not only loved video games, but usually whipped anybody at any game in the arcade. But this time she only shrugged disinterestedly.

Nancy quickly remembered that one of the first things she was told in her Helping Hands training session was that lonely kids often had mood swings. "You want to check out Berrigan's for that jean jacket you said you wanted? I have a friend who works there. Maybe she can get us a good deal."

Nancy stopped midstep, realizing Anna had fallen behind. "Anna," Nancy said gently, "why don't we go somewhere and talk? I can tell something's wrong. I can take you back to my room if you want. That'd be cool! You could meet all my suitemates."

Anna blew a stray strand of hair out of her eyes. When she did, Nancy could see that she'd been crying.

"Maybe not right now," she said tearfully.

Nancy gave Anna's shoulder a supportive squeeze. "You might feel better if you got what's bothering you off your chest."

Anna raised a knuckle to her eye. "Things are kind of tense at home, you know?" she said, squinting up at Nancy.

"Is your dad okay?"

Anna shook her head. "He lost his job."

Nancy swallowed. That explained his car being in the driveway when I came by, she realized.

Anna looked up, a glint of uncertain hope in her eyes. "But Dad keeps telling me there's nothing to worry about," she said. "He's smart, and I know he'll get another job soon and everything will get back to normal."

Nancy nodded. She wanted to be supportive, and she hoped Anna was right, but she had the feeling that she hadn't heard the whole story and that Anna didn't believe her own words.

"I'm hungry," Anna blurted out.

"Again?" Nancy laughed.

Anna smiled wryly. "I didn't eat very much the first time."

Stay positive, Nancy told herself as she led Anna back to Anthony's. At least during the time she spends with you she doesn't have to worry.

"Thank you for shopping at Berrigan's, and please come again," Stephanie said with a sugary smile. She handed a big paper bag over the counter to the older woman she'd been waiting on hand and foot for over an hour.

As soon as the customer had turned the corner, Stephanie's smile evaporated. *"So* annoying."

"You should be happy," Pam said. "You sold her over two hundred dollars' worth of cosmetics."

"And she needs every penny's worth."

Usually that would have gotten a laugh. Stephanie and Pam had a great time rating customers' cosmetics needs on a scale from one to ten. This time, though, Pam didn't laugh or say a thing. Stephanie felt only cold silence as Pam started putting away the dozens of perfume and lipstick samples she'd brought out.

"Nice outfit, by the way," Pam finally said sarcastically. "Jonathan should be pleased."

Stephanie fingered the silky smoothness of her charcoal gray bodysuit. "Why would you say that?"

"You mean, why wouldn't I?" Pam replied darkly.

Stephanie eyed her. "Something on your mind, Pam?"

Pam sprayed the cabinet with glass cleaner and began wiping it down. "I heard what you said about me this morning to Mrs. Caldwell."

Turning her back, Stephanie gave the shelves a few token swipes with a feather duster. "Who told you? Not Alice, by any chance?"

Pam straightened and leveled a scornful stare at Stephanie. "You hate her, don't you? I mean, *really* hate her. You've been looking for a way to make her look bad ever since she nailed you for smoking, and you've finally found it."

Stephanie gave a caustic laugh. "First of all, do

you think I really have the time to plot a way to get back at Alice?"

Pam's voice was pinched and severe: "I'm dying to hear what your second of all is."

"Second of all," Stephanie raised her voice, "I don't care what you think. I didn't take those sweaters. And excuse me for not fawning all over Alice the way you do."

"It's not fawning," Pam shot back. "It's called friendship. Not that you'd know anything about that."

Stephanie was about to tear into Pam when something distracted her: Jonathan Baur.

She quickly composed herself. "Hi," she said with a tense smile.

"Everything all right here?" he asked, looking back and forth between them.

Stephanie shrugged. Pam didn't say a word.

"Isn't it about time for your break, Stephanie?" Jonathan asked.

Stephanie felt a ray of light pierce through this lowly day. "Sure is," she said. "Want to get a cup of coffee?"

"Not right now," he replied, sounding official. He led her aside. "I need to show you something." He handed Stephanie a personal check. "Remember this?"

It had been written that morning by one of Stephanie's customers. "Sure."

"You forgot to initial it," he stated flatly. "And

you didn't take down the customer's phone number."

Stephanie swallowed hard. In the corner of her eye, she could see Pam looking a little too pleased.

"Sorry," she said. "It won't happen again."

"It can't," Jonathan replied. "You have to get it together, Stephanie. I'm willing to give you more time to get the hang of things here. But other people aren't as generous."

Stephanie could feel herself blush. "I understand."

Her eyes swept the floor for something to look at other than Jonathan or Pam. For the first time since she'd arrived at Wilder, Stephanie felt unsure of what to do or say. She'd always prided herself on having a bottomless supply of ammunition for any social situation: a sharp reply, the perfect sniping joke, the cutting, scalding glance. As far as she was concerned, when it came to the all-important topics of fashion and human relations, she was expert.

Now, though, she felt like a complete amateur. Her carefully cultivated exterior was cracking before everyone.

"You look like you could use that break now," Jonathan said more sympathetically.

Stephanie nodded. "I'll just take ten minutes," she said to Pam.

"Don't hurry back," Pam replied coldly.

Wincing at Pam's snub, Stephanie wandered

down the lingerie aisles, absentmindedly fingering the rows of silk and satin. She heard footsteps behind her.

"Don't worry so much about that check." It was Jonathan. "I won't tell anyone. Just be more careful."

Turning, Stephanie leaned back against a shelf. "I know what everybody thinks," she said gloomily. "But I swear I had nothing to do with those sweaters. What I said about finding them on the loading dock is the absolute truth."

Jonathan concentrated his gaze on her. "Tell me more."

Stephanie relayed the complete story of stumbling on the box behind the forklift and how she was going to give it to Alice, but was sure Alice wouldn't believe her. She happened to leave out the part about smoking on the loading dock, but that was beside the point. She didn't want Jonathan to think she was a liar, too—and this was about more than cigarettes.

"So do *you* believe me?" she asked.

"I never thought you were lying," Jonathan replied easily.

"Really?" Stephanie felt a sudden rush of feeling for him.

"The truth is bound to come out sooner or later," Jonathan insisted. "In the meantime, don't do anything that'll get you into any trouble."

Feeling her old confidence surging back, Stephanie raised her right hand. "I'll be the picture of purity and discipline."

Jonathan's dark eyes sparkled, and his mouth curved into a warm, graceful smile that dug dimples into both cheeks. "I don't know about that," he said, laughing easily. "Just no major screwups!"

As Ginny stepped through the doors of the Rock out into the open air, the campus clock tower was chiming. She peered up at the illuminated clock. "Five o'clock!" she said, startled. "Eight straight hours at the library. A new record."

She felt lighter than air, though a little tired. The molecular diagrams she'd been staring at had started to look like connect-the-dot patterns. But at least she was going to ace her organic chem exam in the morning.

Now she was going to do something really smart: give her brain a rest and think of something else.

As she crossed the quad, that something else was Ray. Right about now he's probably sipping tropical drinks next to some record exec's pool, she thought.

Ray and the rest of the band were supposed to take a late flight back into Chicago that night and return to Wilder by taxi—all compliments of Pacific Records.

Swinging her hefty backpack onto her shoulder

and heading toward her dorm, Ginny felt her stomach give a plaintive rumble. Realizing she hadn't eaten all day, she detoured into the Underground.

Everything about the dark little club, from its slightly musty basement smell to the tiny white lights strung along the ceiling, reminded her of Ray. That was where she had first seen him, tall, gaunt, and soulful up on stage, strumming his acoustic guitar and singing one of his haunting songs. That was where she fell in love with him.

Ginny went up to the bar and ordered a sandwich and a soda. While she waited, she looked back toward the corner table where she and Ray liked to sit. I can't wait to hear what happened, she was thinking, when suddenly she saw a familiar face.

"Ray?" Ginny murmured under her breath. She blinked. "Ray!"

There he was, sitting with two of the guys from the band. By the debris covering the table, she could tell that they'd already polished off a nachos supreme.

Ginny didn't get halfway across the club before she was folded in Ray's long arms. Touching her chin, then lifting it, Ray raked his fingers through her long black hair and gave her a kiss that left her breathless.

They'd barely pulled apart when he spoke the words she was dying to hear: "I missed you."

"I was afraid that after all those beautiful

women out there, your memories of me would evaporate," she said.

He shook his head. "I thought about you every minute."

"But why are you back so early?" she asked. "Nothing went wrong, did it?"

Ray gave her a gratified, lopsided grin. "How can anything be wrong when everything is so right?"

"You mean it's all done?" Ginny asked excitedly. "You're signed!"

Ray nodded and this time it was Ginny's turn to envelop him in a hug.

"We wrapped everything up early," Ray explained, "so we caught an earlier plane. I called your suite, but Eileen said you were missing in action at the Rock. Hey, come and have something to eat with us, to celebrate. On Pacific Records, of course. They gave us spending money to cover our expenses."

"Thanks, but I can't even see straight," Ginny said. "I've been studying all day for exams."

"Oh, yeah, those old things," Ray said, and laughed.

Ginny laughed, too, until she saw the expression in Ray's eyes. Exams seemed the furthest thing from his mind. "I hate to be a spoilsport," she said, "but don't forget you have your first one Tuesday morning."

"Sure," he replied buoyantly. "But I'm too

wired to think about it right now. I'll hit the books tonight. Promise."

Ginny raised an eyebrow. "Before or after you give me a proper hello in the privacy of your room?"

"I guess after." Ray smiled, giving her hand a squeeze. "Let me just unwind a little while. Meet you there in a couple hours."

Slinging her book bag over her shoulder, Ginny picked up her sandwich and headed for the door. Before she left she looked back at Ray and the guys sitting and laughing around the table.

He doesn't look like a college student, Ginny mused. He looks like what he is—a guy who just broke out into the real world.

Casting another worried glance at Ray, Ginny smelled trouble. School was a challenge for him. Now how could it be anything but impossible?

Bess didn't know what Casey had just said, but it must have been hilarious, because she was laughing very hard.

She'd just joined Casey and Brian in some lounge chairs in the Student Union. They'd gotten out of their afternoon rehearsal fifteen minutes earlier. Polishing her scenes had turned out to be grueling work, especially after a long morning of studying and a night of not much sleep.

"Bess, you look exhausted," Brian commented.

"But I feel great!" she cried.

"No, you don't," Brian corrected. "You just think you do. You're running on pure adrenaline."

Casey waved her away. "Ignore her. She's just punchy."

Bess hopped to her feet. "Hey, who am I?" she asked. The expression on her face, beautiful and cheerful, instantly shifted into a concentrated mask. Her athletic posture slid into that of someone older, a little hunched. She stroked her chin and looked thoughtfully around the Student Union.

Brian's and Casey's jaws dropped, amazed. "Alan!" they both cried in unison, recognizing the director of their play.

Bess's mind was racing. Something had happened during the last few rehearsals. Just as Casey and Alan Farber had been coaching her to do, she'd stopping *thinking* about her characters so much and started to *feel* them. She had to portray a couple of different characters in the one-acts, and each one had started to inhabit her.

The thing was, she'd had to act out only one of them at a time. Now they were clamoring inside her brain like a crowd.

"Watch this," she said, and took on the role of one of her favorite characters, a bored and angry housewife who by the end of the scene broke out of her dreary life. But instead of reciting lines from the scene, Bess began to improvise, as though her character had walked off the stage and started living a real life in a real home, thinking about real things.

"Bess, that's amazing," Brian said, laughing.

Casey was laughing, too.

Suddenly Bess felt the character inside her shift. She whirled around and, lowering her voice and twisting her expression, became the woman's husband. Taking on the voices of both characters, Bess improvised an entire scene. First they fought, then they made up.

In the corner of her eye, Bess could see that Casey and Brian had slid out to the edges of their seats. They were gazing up at her, happily enjoying her performance.

Everything was clicking. She felt loose, natural, and in command. So this is what it's like, she thought to herself. This is what acting is really supposed to be.

When she finished, Brian and Casey were laughing and shaking their heads. Smiling, Bess took a deep bow.

"We'll call that scene 'True Love,'" Casey said.

"Do another!" Brian commanded.

"I think you should put on a one-woman show," Casey said with a firm nod. "I'm serious. I'm going to talk to Alan about it."

"So talk to me."

Everyone turned. Alan Farber was waving from a couch a few feet away. He was sitting next to a fortyish woman in a long black coat who looked familiar to Bess.

Bess hid her eyes. Farber and the woman must have come in while she was doing her improv.

I never would have done that if I'd known he was there, she thought. Feeling her characters desert her, now she was just Bess Marvin, Wilder freshman. Untalented, hopelessly average, and totally disgraced.

"I can't believe I just did that," she said out loud.

"Why? You were incredible," Casey replied coolly. "And look who he's with."

When Bess dared to look up again, she focused on the woman. Then she swallowed hard. "Oh, no!"

Bess now recognized the woman sitting next to Alan. Her photo had been on the brochure for the New York Institute for Dramatic Arts.

"Jeanne Glasseburg," Casey said.

"And I have just made a complete fool of myself," Bess declared, "and ruined any chance of getting into her class!"

CHAPTER 8

As the six o'clock closing signal rang throughout Berrigan's, Stephanie sighed with relief. "Thank you," she said, and bolted down the stairs, hopefully leaving behind the longest and most grueling day of her life. The only thing left was to endure all those accusing faces in the lounge and locker room. Then freedom!

And studying, she realized with a sorrowful sigh.

Stephanie had her daily escape from the locker room down to a science. Unlock locker, grab jacket, slam locker, and *sayonara!*

But as she shut her locker, she heard someone come over. Stephanie turned.

"Hi, Kristin!" she said, summoning the energy to flash one last smile for the day.

But Kristin didn't look happy. In fact, she had the same worried, paranoid look everyone else around Berrigan's was wearing these days.

"I just thought you might want to know that I overheard Alice and Mrs. Caldwell talking a few minutes ago," Kristin said.

"No doubt about me," Stephanie said, tossing her head.

"There's been another incident," Kristin went on dismally. "Alice was double-checking all the shipping orders that went through today, and she found one from cosmetics that was shipped to the wrong address."

Stephanie rolled her eyes. "Oh, let me guess."

Kristin nodded. "Your signature was on it."

"Well, that's funny," Stephanie said acidly, "because I didn't make out a single shipping order today."

"Stephanie."

Stephanie turned to find Jonathan and Mrs. Caldwell standing in front of them. Jonathan looked anxious and was shifting his weight from foot to foot.

"Come with us for a second?" Mrs. Caldwell asked.

"Good luck," Kristin whispered as Stephanie followed them to ordering and shipping.

Alice was sitting behind her desk. She pointed at a single piece of paper before her.

"Is this yours?" Mrs. Caldwell asked.

Stephanie looked at it. It was a shipping order,

dated that day. And the signature at the bottom was hers!

"Yes," Stephanie said, shocked. "I mean, *no!*" She turned to Jonathan. She knew he'd believe her. "That's my signature, but I have no idea how it got there."

"Simple," Alice said bitingly. "You put it there."

Stephanie shook her head in protest. "No way. I didn't have any shipping orders today. There has to be a mistake."

"And you made it," Alice cut in, "the second you decided to set me up and ruin my credibility with this company."

Stephanie pointed at the order. She had a thousand venomous things she wanted to say to Alice, and all but one would have gotten her fired on the spot. *"I'm* the one being set up," she finally sputtered.

In the corner of her eye, she saw Mrs. Caldwell arch an eyebrow with surprise. Jonathan was grim and silent.

Alice let out a rueful laugh. "That's a good one, Stephanie. That really is. But I think you should know that the customer who was supposed to have received this order never got it. I checked the driver's log and this order wasn't listed. It never made it out of the store. Four hundred dollars' worth of merchandise." Alice stopped for a moment and stared at Stephanie, then she continued.

"Between the sweaters that were almost stolen, and this merchandise that *was* stolen, we're not talking about little errors in judgment anymore. Now we're talking about a crime. And not just larceny. There's malicious mischief and vandalism, too. Mr. Berrigan said that he will be calling the police tomorrow."

Mouth agape, Stephanie turned from face to face. "And you think it's me? Why would *I* do it? I *need* this job!"

Alice brought her hands together, her face the picture of self-satisfaction. "And why would *I?* This is my career. For you, this job is merely to earn a little extra spending money."

Fists clenched, eyes blazing, Stephanie stared Alice down. "If you think I did this, then prove it!"

"Oh, I will," Alice replied icily. "I will."

Strolling slowly back to his apartment on Waterman Street, Jake should have been feeling great. He'd had his most productive day of studying all semester. It was Sunday evening, which meant an Italian dinner with his roommates Nick and Dennis, followed by a game of poker. The perfect way to prepare for another hectic week.

But Jake wasn't feeling great. In fact, something had been nagging at him all day. Pulling his woolen jacket tight against the chill, he replayed for the hundredth time how on his way to the Rock that morning he'd passed by Java Joe's and spotted Nancy at her usual corner booth. He was about to go in and say hello when he saw she wasn't alone. She was with Terry Schneider.

"Talking," Jake said out loud, trying to convince himself. "And practically snuggled together," he had to admit.

Terry had been crouched over the table, and Nancy was looking up at him with what seemed to Jake to be adoration. Then she'd reached out and touched him.

"Couldn't be," Jake grumbled as he slowly climbed the steps to his apartment. "You had a bad angle."

But he just couldn't chase out of his mind the thought of how excited Nancy had been lately about the film society. And how good-looking Terry was. And, though he hated to admit it, how much attention Nancy seemed to be paying him lately.

What was worse, about a week ago, Terry had asked Jake a lot of probing questions about him and Nancy, such as how close they really were, as though he was thinking about asking Nancy out himself.

Putting his key in the lock of his door, Jake finally put the question to himself he'd been avoiding all day. Is Terry Schneider the reason Nancy's been acting so weird?

The living room of his apartment was dim and silent. As far as Jake could tell, Nick and Dennis had stopped talking midsentence. Sitting on overstuffed chairs, they both had surprised, interrupted expressions on their faces.

"Hi!" Nick said too happily.

"What's up?" Dennis asked.

Jake eyed them both. "Is *everybody* on campus acting bizarre, or is it just me?"

Nick and Dennis shrugged. "Just you, old buddy," Nick said, and laughed.

Jake nodded resignedly. "That's what I thought. You order the food?"

Dennis grabbed at the phone. "We were waiting for you."

"You never wait," Jake replied suspiciously. "In fact, I'm lucky if there's anything left for me."

"Well," Nick said hesitantly, "Dennis and I were deep in conversation."

"No kidding," Jake remarked, lowering his book bag to the floor and peeling off his coat.

Dennis ordered the food, gave their address, and hung up. "Now about the couch," he said. "The one you're going to pick out for us."

Jake shook his head clear. "Do I know about this?"

"You do now," Nick said. "That old thing in the corner is about to collapse."

Jake cocked his head. "It's been collapsing for months. Why the rush?"

"Because we finally have the money to pitch in to get a new one," Dennis said.

"Okay, sounds good to me," Jake said, kicking

his feet up onto the overturned crate they used for a coffee table. "When's the big day?"

Dennis and Nick exchanged looks. "Funny you should mention it," Nick said with a glint in his eye. "We thought that of the three of us, you are definitely the only one in possession of enough good taste to make such a weighty decision."

"We don't care what it looks like," Dennis added confidently. "As long as it's comfortable."

Jake was laughing. "Okay, okay, I get the picture. I'll take Nancy with me. She's the one with the great taste."

Nick gave a double thumbs-up.

But just mentioning Nancy's name cued up in Jake's mind the picture of Nancy and Terry from that morning.

"Be right back," he said, preoccupied. He headed for his room and closed the door. Without reaching for a light, he dialed Nancy's number. It was so natural, he didn't even have to think.

"Hey," he said when she picked up.

"There you are," Nancy replied cheerfully. "I was wondering when you were going to call. I was about to send out a rescue party—of one, of course."

Instantly Jake's pulse quickened. It was so rare when things weren't great between them that he felt awkward when there was the slightest hitch.

"We have a mission," Jake said with mock solemnity, and relayed the story of the search for the new couch.

Nancy was laughing. "Sure, why not," she said. "Maybe tomorrow afternoon. Then we can hang out together and study."

"Sounds terrific," Jake replied, relieved and surprised that she was so willing to see him all of a sudden.

He cleared his throat, and even in the dark he could feel himself blush with apprehension. "You know, I saw you in Java Joe's this morning on the way to the Rock—"

Nancy hesitated. "You did?"

"And Terry, too," Jake added, the casualness draining from his voice. "You guys were hanging out. Talking hot and heavy, it looked like."

"Oh, Jake, you're not *jealous,* are you?" Nancy laughed.

"Jealous?" Jake replied quickly, as if it was the most ludicrous thing in the world.

But deep inside him, his stomach leaped. That wasn't the typical light and airy Nancy Drew laugh. It was a little forced, a little nervous. If being an investigative reporter had taught Jake anything, it was how to read someone's tone of voice. How to get the story behind the story.

And this story didn't feel like it had a happy ending.

"See you tomorrow," Jake said dejectedly, and cut the line.

But he didn't put down the phone. He held

on to it, as if it would tell him what he wanted to know.

"You're hiding something," he said under his breath.

As Nancy put down the phone, she sighed with troubled relief.

"Is he catching on?" Kara asked. Hunched over her desk, she lifted her head over the books she'd arranged like blinders on either side of her. Trails of paper crisscrossed both of their beds. Empty soda cans and bags of chips littered the floor.

Nancy shook her head. "But he's getting close. He saw Terry and me talking today. Terry's helping me get a present for Jake. I think Jake believes I actually have something going on with Terry. Can you imagine?"

Kara stared at her blankly. "Uh, yeah. Terry's hot."

Nancy shot Kara a mock glare. "But Jake's hotter. And smarter. And more fun—"

Kara held up her hands in surrender. "Okay, okay, I get the picture. Jake's the most attractive male on earth. Back to work."

Nancy slipped out of her jeans and sweater and into her new study uniform: maroon sweats with the Wilder Norsemen mascot stenciled in white, gold, and black. She tied back her long strawberry blond hair with a scrunchie and flipped on her computer.

Waiting for it to boot up, she shuffled the note-cards she had in her hands and tried to psych herself to study.

There was a knock at the door.

"Go away!" Kara moaned.

Reva burst in, pencils behind both ears. "I need a floppy disk. Got an extra?"

Nancy handed one over.

"How's the big party coming?" Reva asked.

"Fine, fine. 'Bye, Reva."

Kara waved from behind her barricade.

"Okay, okay," Reva said, feigning dejection. "Later."

A minute didn't pass before there was another knock.

Kara groaned.

"I need to draw a portrait for my art class assignment," came a voice. It was Eileen's. "Anybody want to just lie in bed and pose? You can even sleep."

"Don't tempt me," Nancy muttered. "Sorry."

Five minutes later the door was rattling.

Kara sat up. "I will *scream*."

"No one's here!" Nancy called.

But the door flew open. Stephanie was standing there, looking a little harried.

Nancy rolled her eyes. "Stephanie, I have one night to write this paper. I haven't gotten a thing done all day. Can this wait, whatever it is?"

Ignoring her, Stephanie closed the door behind

her and lowered herself onto Nancy's bed, scattering her notes.

"Stephanie!" Nancy yelled. She was about to get annoyed until she looked closer at Stephanie's face.

Stephanie was usually impeccably made up. For the first time since Nancy had known her, though, Stephanie looked like a wreck. Her mascara was smudged, her hair messy. Her stare seemed unfocused and nervous.

"Stephanie?" Nancy inquired, concerned.

Stephanie looked Nancy straight in the eyes. "Nancy," she said pleadingly, "I need your help."

CHAPTER 9

It was ten o'clock, and despite the Zetas' reputation for round-the-clock games of pool and darts, the frat house was surprisingly still and quiet. Bess had run into Paul's roommate, Emmet, heading to the Rock hours ago, so she knew Paul was alone.

Still, climbing the three flights of stairs to his room, Bess couldn't shake the gloomy feeling that she'd blown her chance at Glasseburg's acting class.

Wincing, she recalled most of the routine she'd made up for Brian and Casey. You're such an amateur! she berated herself.

Standing outside Paul's room, Bess knocked on the door, and Paul called back, "Who is it?" Bess smiled. Sometimes just the sound of his voice had the power to chase away her worries.

"It's me," she said.

When the door swung open, Bess found a guy whose short blond hair—usually neatly combed—now looked a mess. He wore a ragged T-shirt and old gym shorts.

"Ooh, attractive," she said sarcastically.

Paul shrugged. "Study outfit. Like it?"

"Love it."

Bess stepped in, giving him an affectionate pinch as she went by.

Her relationship with Paul had deepened over the past few weeks. They'd always been incredibly attracted to each other, but every time she saw him lately, she had her breath taken away. It was more than the way he looked, she realized. She could tell they were really falling for each other, heart, soul, and all.

Though right now, the only thing Bess felt like falling into was a deep depression.

"I'm such a dope," she complained, sitting down on Paul's bed.

"What now?" Paul asked, sitting beside her.

"Remember Jeanne Glasseburg?"

Paul squinted with mock uncertainty. "I seem to recall that name—"

The truth was, Bess had been talking of practically no one else since Friday.

"Okay, so I haven't shut up about her," Bess went on. "Well, listen to this."

Bess described how exhausted she, Brian, and Casey were, and how punchy they'd gotten after rehearsal. As Bess went into detail about how she'd improvised the characters from her scenes in the one-acts, Paul scooted back against his pile of pillows. Nodding, grinning, he listened with rapt attention. "Casey's right," he said. "It sounds like you were amazing."

Bess waved her hands. "No, no, stop! You don't understand. *You* may think it was cool, and maybe it actually was kind of funny. But guess who else witnessed my little performance? Alan Farber and Jeanne Glasseburg! They were sitting there, too, and I didn't know it!"

"Excellent!" Paul said enthusiastically.

Bess was totally confused. "Excellent?"

"Don't you see?" Paul pointed out. "You had your audition for the class and you don't even know it! Which means that you were probably more relaxed and did a lot better than you would have done in a real audition."

Bess was thoughtful. The smallest flicker of a smile tugged at the corners of her lips. "Really, you think so?"

Paul nodded firmly. "Now come here."

Bess slid back, leaned into Paul's arms, and buried her face in his neck. She took in the way she felt in his hands, the way he smelled, the way he touched her. She closed her eyes, transported to a place she hadn't been before, someplace eternally warm and safe, where nothing was important except their happiness.

"Don't ever leave," she said, her head on his chest.

"Where would I go?" Paul asked. "What would I ever do without you?"

"Hmm, me, too." She looked up and pressed a finger against his chest. "You know you always manage to find a way to cheer me up when I'm down. I feel as though I can talk to you about anything."

"You can."

Bess began to stroke his hair, feeling the silky smoothness of each strand between her fingers.

"Sometimes," she said quietly, reaching up to touch his face, "I feel as if you brought me to life."

Gently Paul lifted her chin and bowed his head. His lips on hers were supple and warm. Just like Paul himself. He's everything I could want, everything I need, she thought happily as the strength of his kiss intensified.

Their romantic mood was shattered by the scrape of the door opening. Bess sprang from Paul's arms.

"Sorry, did I interrupt?"

It was Emmet, his face in full blush.

"Not at all," Paul said tightly.

Bess straightened her sweater. As much as she liked Emmet, she sort of wished he would just vaporize—for another hour or so, anyway.

"How'd it go with Eileen today?" Paul asked.

Bess straightened up, suddenly interested. "That's right. The art opening."

"The art opening," Emmet moaned. He shook his head. "I may not be an artist like she is, but even I know that wasn't art."

"I detect a less than enlightening experience," Bess said lightheartedly.

Emmet nodded sadly and gave them a blow-by-blow account of his latest episode of foot in mouth.

"At least you were honest," Paul concluded with a shrug. "That has to count for something."

Emmet smirked. "Yeah, for points toward the Ignorant Dumb Jock of the Year award."

He stripped off his jacket, dropped his backpack to the floor, and draped himself over Paul's desk chair. Much to Bess's dismay, he looked as though he was going to stay awhile.

But then, Bess could never resist a sappy love story. The fact was, Emmet and Eileen seemed perfect for each other. They just didn't know it yet, and Bess wished she could help them somehow.

"There's only one thing to do," Bess said decisively. "You and Eileen have to have a real heart-to-heart."

"We do?" Emmet replied.

"I wouldn't apologize for the way you feel," Paul added, "but if you think you keep coming off sounding dumb, you need to show her you're not. Honesty looks smart. And if she doesn't like who you really are, then maybe it isn't meant to be."

Emmet was nodding, his eyes registering Paul's comment.

"That's exactly what I think," Bess agreed with a nod.

"I'll give it a try," Emmet said. "It couldn't get much worse, anyway."

Bess glanced back toward Paul. He gave her a wink and a knowing smile.

It's as if he's inside my brain sometimes, she thought to herself. As if he knows what I'm feeling and what I'm going to say. It's scary it feels so right. I'll never be alone now. No matter where I am, he'll always be with me.

"Ray, come on over here and sit with me," Ginny said lovingly.

But Ray sat as solid and immovable as a statue on his dorm-room desk, picking out a few rhythms on his guitar. He'd been perched there for over an hour, improvising melodies and telling Ginny about L.A.

Ginny, meanwhile, sat on his bed, trying to make sense of the chaos of his books and notes.

"Ray, you have an exam in a little more than twenty-four hours," Ginny pointed out.

"Here, listen," Ray interrupted excitedly. "What do you think of this?"

Ginny watched mesmerized as Ray's fingers worked like spiders over the guitar's neck. The new riff was haunting and beautiful. "I want you to write lyrics to it when it's done," he said.

Ginny felt a rush of pride at how they'd learned to work together. Before this year, she hadn't even known she could write songs. But Ray had drawn deep emotions out of her. As magical as he was at playing a wood guitar, Ray had become an expert at playing her heart. Around him, she was like a flesh-and-blood instrument.

And the results were hard to believe. Some of Pacific Records' favorite songs from the Beat Poets had been the ones with Ginny's lyrics!

"It's beautiful, Ray," Ginny said. "But why do I get the feeling that I'm the only one getting any work done around here?"

Ray shrugged. "I *am* working. This is work, real work. And this is what I love."

Ginny sighed. "I know," she said sympathetically. "No one supports your music as much as I do. But there are also things you have to do, so that you can keep doing things you love to do."

"Now that we have this contract, though," Ray replied between runs of harmonic scales, "I sort of have to do this."

Ginny sighed exasperatedly. She knew she had to say something. "You're so smart, Ray," she started gingerly, "but if you don't study, your grades are going way south."

Ray played on, as if he hadn't heard a word.

"And when that happens?" she continued. "If you flunk these tests, you might go on academic probation. You might be asked to leave." Ginny's throat tightened with emotion. "And then what happens to us?" she asked.

Ray stopped playing. He put down his guitar and sat next to her on the bed. "What happens to us is more of the same," he said, taking her hands. "I love you. Being a student at Wilder or not isn't going to change that. Ever."

But all Ginny could hear was "or not." "Ray, what do you mean 'or not'?" she asked fearfully.

Ray nodded resignedly. "I actually wanted to talk to you about that."

Ginny braced herself. She knew when she dropped him off at the airport on Friday that this could happen.

"This past weekend in L.A.," Ray said, "I talked to lots of musicians. All of them had dropped whatever they were doing to work on their music. Some of them starved for years until they made it. I know it's harsh, but starting out in this business is a twenty-four-hour-a-day job."

Blinking away tears, Ginny looked dead ahead. Whatever happens, don't cry, she commanded herself.

"So," Ray went on, "what I guess I'm trying to say is, I've been thinking it through, and I'm kind of thinking about dropping out of Wilder—"

Ginny knew what came next. She moved her lips to the words—*and moving to L.A.*

"And moving to L.A.," Ray said.

Nancy's watch alarm started bleeping.

"What's that?" Stephanie asked.

"Midnight." Nancy yawned. "That was to wake me up if I fell asleep while I was working on my paper. Fat chance of that."

Stephanie was sprawled across Nancy's bed, her hands behind her head, Nancy's notecards kicked to the floor. Nancy, her feet up on her desk, was playing absentmindedly with her computer mouse. Kara had fallen asleep at her desk over an hour ago.

"So much for handing *you* in on time," Nancy lamented, looking at her computer screen and the text of the paper she'd been working on.

"Come *on!*" Stephanie sat bolt upright. Much to Nancy's dismay, she showed no signs of fatigue. If anything, she was more worked up and determined than ever. "Where are your priorities? This is about my life. I have a real problem here."

"You're right, Steph," Nancy said, biting her tongue. "Forgive me. It's not like I have to worry about grades or anything."

"Good deeds are always rewarded," Stephanie assured her.

That surprised Nancy, coming from Stephanie.

Maybe she's learning something from this mess, Nancy thought.

"So what do you think?" Stephanie asked anxiously.

Nancy sighed. "Okay. So yesterday you were sure that Alice had screwed up that sweater order and tried to cover herself by pinning it on you, right?"

"Because she's jealous of me," Stephanie added earnestly. "Don't forget that."

Nancy had to laugh. "Oh, no fear of that. Though she wouldn't be alone."

"Of course not," Stephanie replied blithely.

"And as for this shipping order thing today, maybe Alice made *another* mistake and somehow got your signature on the order to cover herself?"

Stephanie nodded, though less certainly. "Maybe," she said.

"You don't sound convinced," Nancy said.

Stephanie shrugged. "Look, Alice is the enemy. She's over the hill, and she's stuck all day like a hermit in the bowels of that boring store. So she hates me, all right? But I guess she's not dumb."

"And her record has been perfect until now," Nancy pointed out. "Not to mention Berrigan's spotless reputation."

Stephanie snorted. "So they say."

Nancy chewed on the end of her pencil. "So."

"But if it's not Alice, who is it?" Stephanie wanted to know.

"Someone who wants to make the ordering and shipping department look bad. And who doesn't mind using you to do it," Nancy surmised. "Maybe when you found those sweaters behind the forklift, you gave our mystery person a good idea."

Nancy could practically see Stephanie's mind churning, running down her list of enemies, weighing the possibilities.

In frustration, Stephanie reached for something, ended up with Nancy's notebook, and heaved it across the room. "I'll kill them if they blow this job for me!" she shrieked.

Kara lifted her head off her desk. "What? Who?"

"Go back to sleep," Stephanie sniped. She turned to Nancy, her face set with determination. "But how could my signature end up on that shipping order if I didn't put it there? The only things I signed today were sales receipts."

"Positive?" Nancy asked. "Did anybody give you something else to sign today, like a payroll receipt or a tax form?"

Stephanie concentrated, then cocked her head as if she'd remembered something. "There was something," she said. "But it couldn't be."

"What couldn't be?" Nancy prodded her.

"That sales receipt I spaced out on." Stephanie turned to Nancy, her piercing black eyes wide open with worry. "Jonathan brought it up to me."

"*The* Jonathan?"

Stephanie nodded. "I didn't even look at it. I just signed where he said to sign." Suddenly, Stephanie was waving her hands and shaking her head. "No way. Just no way, okay? He likes me. He worships the ground I walk on. Or he will, anyway, in another few days. He's on *my* side!"

"Okay, so Jonathan's out," Nancy said to appease her, though she refused to count him out. "Who else?"

"Well, Pam and I haven't exactly been getting along," Stephanie said offhandedly. "She keeps taking Alice's side."

Nancy looked at Stephanie. Stephanie, lips pursed, shook her head no.

"No way," they both said in unison.

"Pam's too cool," Nancy said.

"Well, I don't know about *that*," Stephanie countered. "But I doubt she'd go to these lengths to get back at me."

Nancy made a big show of looking at her watch and slapping her thighs, hoping Stephanie would get the message. "Okay," she said, yawning and stretching. "I still have eight hours to write my paper."

Stephanie eyed her dubiously. "Oh, was I interrupting?"

Nancy laughed. "Of course not, Steph. I'll tell you what. I'll swing by Berrigan's tomorrow to see what I can find out myself. But keep your eyes open. And no smoking on the loading dock!"

Stephanie saluted. "Aye-aye."

"Now get out of here. I haven't flunked Western Civ yet."

At the door Stephanie stopped and turned around. "Oh, and Nancy," she said hesitantly. She searched the room with her eyes, obviously struggling with what she wanted to say. "Thanks."

The door shut. As Nancy started picking notecards off the floor, it struck her how vulnerable and nervous Stephanie seemed. Though she had to admit, nervousness was kind of attractive on her.

Maybe I didn't give her enough credit, Nancy considered. Maybe Ms. Keats is more complicated than we all thought.

CHAPTER 10

Hmmm, Casey thought, smiling dreamily. Sounds great. I guess I should write this down. But I like my fantasies better.

It was Monday morning, and Casey was in her literature class, gazing at the front of the room with a rapt expression on her face. The professor was lecturing on a particularly romantic novel from the early 1900s. And Casey had been daydreaming, substituting herself and the very handsome male student who sat next to her for the two lovers in the story.

What did he just say about that plot point? Casey wondered, panicking for a second. I really should take notes.

But Casey was having a hard time pulling her attention from the good-looking guy next to her.

Was he new? Casey hadn't really noticed him before.

But how could I have missed him, Casey wondered to herself, her chin on her hand. He's so *hot*.

Just then everyone in class started laughing.

Casey wondered what the joke had been. She glanced around the room, and then she froze.

The professor was staring right at her, a look of icy disapproval on her face. Suddenly Casey realized she was the only one not taking any notes. Not to mention the fact that she'd been practically drooling over the guy next to her.

Casey sat up and grabbed her pen. She started scribbling away in her notebook, hardly paying attention to what she was writing.

What's my problem? Casey wondered. I've been in this class all year and I never even looked twice at this guy. So why all of a sudden does he look so incredibly cute?

Casey glanced around the room. Strangely enough, lots of guys in her class had become terribly appealing in one way or another—one had an adorable little smile, one had incredible green eyes, one even had a little scar on his cheek that Casey thought was mysterious.

Oh, no! Casey thought. Am I just noticing them because they're all off-limits now?

Casey could feel her face turning red. She was sure that it was obvious that she'd just scoped out every single guy in the class.

I've got to get a grip! Casey realized. I've got the most gorgeous, most fabulous guy in the world, who wants to spend the rest of his life with me.

There's only one gorgeous face you need to remember, Casey told herself. "And that's Charley's," she whispered, as she kept her eyes glued to her desk.

At 8:55 A.M. Nancy was pulling away from the social sciences department in her Mustang. She'd made the deadline for her paper with five minutes to spare. Checking traffic in her rearview mirror, she caught a glimpse of herself and grimaced.

She'd managed to grab a shower before she left the dorm, but she couldn't wash away her bloodshot eyes.

"You really look like you didn't get any sleep," she told herself.

But at least she'd handed in her paper.

That done, Nancy took a big swallow of her coffee and headed downtown toward Berrigan's. An hour earlier as she printed out her paper, she'd had a stroke of genius. She wanted to poke around the store to see what she could learn about Stephanie's problem, but she couldn't do it as a customer. So she'd called the personnel manager, Mrs. Caldwell, and explained she was a business major doing a research paper on the competition between successful smaller family-owned businesses like Berrigan's and the huge chains.

Mrs. Caldwell was only too happy to have her down. And when Nancy said she was particularly interested in the ordering and shipping department, which everyone knew was the key to Berrigan's success, Mrs. Caldwell agreed to allow her to interview Alice Woodward.

"Not a bad cover, Drew," she said self-approvingly as she pulled into Berrigan's lot behind the store. "And after an all-nighter, too."

Inside the store, the first person she saw was Kristin, Pam's friend. She seemed friendly and easy to talk to.

"Hey," Nancy said.

Kristin was inspecting a display of handbags hanging off a faux tree. She looked at Nancy without a glimmer of recognition. "May I help you?" she asked distractedly.

"Kristin? Nancy, remember? Pam and Stephanie's friend?"

Kristin grabbed at Nancy's hand. "Sorry," she apologized. "Since that night things here at the store have been kind of tense. Everyone's on edge."

"Sorry to hear that. But do you think you could point me toward ordering and shipping?"

"The belly of the beast," Kristin joked. "Sure you want to go down there?"

Nancy smiled reassuringly. "Just doing some research for a paper."

Heading for the stairs, Kristin suddenly stopped. Nancy followed her gaze toward a tall young man who was as well dressed and as perfectly proportioned as a mannequin.

"Let me guess," Nancy began. "That's—"

Kristin nodded. "Stephanie has practically branded him hers. Just let Stephanie catch you looking at him with any interest at all, and you're dead."

Nancy laughed easily. "Well, he is attractive."

"Gorgeous," Kristin said, and sighed audibly. "Steph's kind of territorial."

"Yeah, like a pterodactyl," Kristin bantered. "Anyway, the door you're looking for is at the bottom of those stairs. Alice should be in there. She always is."

"Thanks," Nancy said, and headed downstairs.

The door stenciled Ordering and Shipping was open. Inside, behind a desk, sat a serious-looking woman leafing through sales receipts, counting silently to herself.

So this is big, bad Alice, Nancy thought to herself.

Behind the woman hung a huge montage of best-wishes cards and photos showing Alice posing with a host of other employees.

Not an unpopular woman, Nancy surmised, only strengthening her doubts that Alice was behind Stephanie's frame-up.

"You must be from the university," the woman said.

Nancy nodded. "I'm Nancy Drew. Ms. Woodward, right?"

"Yes, I've been expecting you. Please sit down," Alice said, offering her hand. "What can I do for you today?"

Nancy described her fake research project and asked Alice to explain Berrigan's famous shipping procedures.

"Easy," Alice said, without a trace of concern with what had been going on. She detailed how when a shipping order was taken in a department, the merchandise with the sales slip attached was brought down and stored on shelves in the shipping area next door. Except, of course, for large furniture, which was sent directly to the loading dock while the slip came to her department. Then the merchandise was packed for shipment by a small crew that was always on call.

"So, any employee coming through here or working in ordering and shipping has total access."

Nancy thought she detected suspicion in Alice's eyes. "Don't mind me," she said cheerfully. "I'm just comparing systems in my brain. Berrigan's is light-years better than anyone else's!"

"Thank you," Alice replied. "We try. Would you like to see some of our orders being loaded at the loading docks?"

"Definitely," Nancy said, beating Alice to her feet.

As Alice led her on a quick tour, Nancy ticked

off in her mind all the things that Stephanie had told her about. There were the forklifts, and the shelves where the merchandise sat waiting to be loaded. And back inside, the infamous locker room.

"Everything seems to work like clockwork," Nancy said reverently.

"We try to do that," Alice said with a nod. "Though that makes my job harder. I'm usually in my office over an hour after everyone else has gone home, combing through the paperwork for the day's orders. Sometimes there's so much to keep track of it's overwhelming."

"It must take a lot of concentration," Nancy said.

"You can say that again," Alice said with a laugh that meant Nancy had no idea how much.

"And you probably have to shut out the outside world," Nancy continued, leading her on.

Alice shrugged. "I hadn't thought of it that way, but I suppose you're right. When I'm in that office counting, a bomb could go off out here and I wouldn't notice."

Ideas were rising so fast in Nancy's brain that she was having trouble keeping up.

With Alice buried back there at the end of the day, she realized, someone who wanted to sabotage the orders would have the perfect opportunity to do it, not to mention change orders that hadn't been sent out yet and were just sitting on the shelves.

127

Addresses could be changed, Nancy mused. Then something struck her: Signatures could be added. Signatures like Stephanie's . . .

"Can you wait here a second?" Alice asked. She was chatting with a sales clerk, who had asked her to check on an order.

"Sure, go ahead," Nancy replied. Drifting back into Alice's office, she walked behind Alice's desk. She quickly scanned the bulletin board. It was like a complete history of Alice Woodward. Pictures of a young Alice at home with her parents. Standing in front of various stores.

Nancy's eyes suddenly stopped on a particular picture of Alice standing in front of the entrance to Dancor's, one of Berrigan's biggest competitors. "Wow, she's even worked for the competition," Nancy thought out loud, impressed. Then she remembered what Kristin had said the other night about her father working at Dancor's.

Maybe Alice knew him, Nancy wondered.

As Nancy strolled back outside, she noticed a blur of clothing ducking into a doorway. Alice was nowhere in sight, so Nancy casually followed and stopped outside the doorway.

Tall, dark, and handsome, Nancy thought, as she watched Stephanie's latest human target, Jonathan Baur. His back to her, he was pacing in front of the shelves of merchandise waiting to be shipped out. He started fingering the packages, as if he were looking for something but wouldn't know what it was until he found it. Then he grabbed a few packages and lifted them, sizing them up and inspecting their sales slips.

"Nancy, sorry I got pulled away," Alice called behind her. She had two cups of coffee in her hands and offered one to Nancy. "Now, where were we?"

"Right here," Nancy said distractedly.

Her pulse quickened. She couldn't take her eyes off Jonathan. At the sound of Alice's voice, he'd stiffened and jammed a sales order slip back into the shelves, between two packages as if he were hiding something.

Or doing something wrong, Nancy thought.

Then Jonathan quickly stepped through a back door and was gone.

"What else can I show you?" Alice was asking.

"Nothing," Nancy replied, pursuing Jonathan with her eyes as he came around the corner and passed them. "Nothing at all."

This is exactly what you needed, Eileen told herself as she felt herself hit her running stride. The rhythmic sound of her running on the gravel path was incredibly soothing.

She'd been dying all through her last class of the day to get down to the boathouse to stretch her legs. Now that she was here and clearing her mind, she couldn't remember a thing about the test she'd just taken, and she just didn't care.

There was something else Eileen needed to think about—and his name was Emmet Lehman.

He should be perfect for me, she mused.

But then she replayed how things were between them every time they'd gotten together, and it seemed like a lost cause. The truth was, Emmet had really bothered her the other day at the exhibit. It wasn't so much that he'd embarrassed her. She was hurt because Emmet didn't respect what she did. If he thought art was so stupid, didn't that mean he thought she was stupid, too?

Maybe it's just one of those chemistry things, she mused.

Though the chemistry had seemed the one really good thing, Eileen admitted to herself, recalling how attracted she had been to Emmet.

Eileen spotted another runner coming toward her from the other side of the lake.

"Another nutty jock," Eileen said. Who else would come out for a pleasure run in forty-degree weather?

The other runner had just rounded the end of the lake, and Eileen could finally make him out. Defensively she clenched her fists.

It was Emmet.

Eileen knew she was still running, but all of a sudden she felt as if her body was moving in slow motion. Of all the people to see, she thought, feeling confused. Was it fate? Or just really bad luck?

Just then Emmet looked up from the path. Eileen noticed him slow down when he saw her.

Eileen didn't know what to do. It was like a bad movie. They could have been the only people in the world.

But if this was a movie, Eileen thought, we'd run right into each other's arms and everything would be solved.

They both came to a stop on the gravel path, face-to-face for the first time since the disastrous art opening. There were ten feet between them, but it could have been miles.

Eileen nodded, waiting to see if Emmet would say anything. But instead, he just stood there, his breath coming out in frosty little clouds. His arms hanging at his sides.

Eileen caught her breath in her throat. Emmet really was handsome—exactly the kind of guy she'd always pictured herself with when she would daydream about having a boyfriend. His blond hair was dark and damp from his run, and his cheeks were red with cold. He should have been perfect. Hadn't everyone said so?

Sighing, Eileen glanced down at her shoes. When she looked up again, she caught Emmet's eye. Her heart stopped in her chest.

Emmet's blue eyes seemed to be full of the same confusion she was battling, a heartbreaking mix of hurt and anger. Eileen was about to turn away when she saw another emotion flicker across his face.

Could it be what she thought? For one minute, Eileen was sure he'd looked hopeful.

"Emmet," Eileen said tentatively.

Emmet snapped his head up.

"Yes?" he asked, and Eileen knew she'd been right.

Things hadn't worked out so far, but somehow Eileen just wasn't ready to give up.

"Well," Eileen said, blowing into her hands and stamping her feet. "I was just wondering—"

"Yes?" Emmet said again, stepping toward her.

"I mean, I don't know if you're up to it," Eileen began.

"Another art opening?" Emmet asked painfully.

"No." Eileen smiled. "I was thinking of something you might have a chance at."

"Oh," Emmet said, his face falling. "And what would that be?"

"How about a race?" Eileen asked. "Back to the boathouse."

Emmet seemed surprised, but then a smile spread over his face. "You're on! And you think I just might have a chance?"

"Well," Eileen said, "I guess we'll have to wait and see."

Before Emmet could reply, Eileen turned around and took off.

"Hey!" she heard Emmet calling. "That wasn't a fair start."

"Fair, shmair!" Eileen chuckled. Then she put

her head down and began sprinting as fast as she could.

There was no way she was going to slow down. Emmet was a star running back, after all.

Eileen was right. Seconds later all she heard was the sound of Emmet's shoes pounding the gravel path behind her.

CHAPTER 11

"Don't move, and empty your pockets."

Jake raised his arms in surrender. "Take my wallet. Take everything. Take me."

He turned and Nancy stepped into his arms, burying her nose in the crook of his neck.

She'd just left her car in the Thayer parking lot and was heading toward the entrance to her dorm, where she'd found Jake standing with his hands jammed in his pockets.

"Where have you been the last few days?" Jake asked, only half-kidding.

Nancy knew what he meant. She was keeping a secret, but it wasn't what he thought. Now Wednesday's party was getting close. She couldn't let up on him now.

"Oh, here and there," she said elusively, then

flashed him a thousand-watt smile. "I'm here now. But I was just at Berrigan's."

"Really? A prestudy shop?"

"I wish," Nancy replied, nodding toward the door. "Come on in. I have to get my books before we go."

With their arms around each other's waists, they headed for the stairs.

"I was kind of doing some research for Stephanie," Nancy said.

"Is she paying you to write a paper?" Jake asked.

Nancy laughed. "Not yet. Actually she's in a lot of trouble."

"Uh-huh," Jake said, unimpressed.

Nancy knew that Jake thought of Stephanie as a necessary evil to be avoided at all costs if possible. But Nancy had been starting to see glimmers of another Stephanie.

"No, listen to this," she persisted.

As they climbed the two flights of stairs to the third floor of Nancy's suite, Nancy filled Jake in on what had been going on at Berrigan's and how Stephanie was being framed.

"Stephanie's a lot of things, but she's no thief," Nancy finished saying.

They were standing outside the door to her suite.

"Uh-huh," Jake said, still unimpressed .

"And this manager she's into, Jonathan," Nancy continued, "I've never seen her feel like that about any guy before."

"Like a predator, you mean," Jake quipped.

Nancy shook her head. "When I ran into her before I left the store this morning and told her how I caught Jonathan doing something weird with the sales receipts, she got incredibly upset. No way it's Jonathan framing her, she said. Whatever she's feeling, it's different. It's deep."

"I'll believe it when I see it," Jake replied. "But right now, it's study time." He eyed her, troubled. "But are you up for it?"

Nancy lolled her head. "It's that obvious?"

"Well, the dark circles under your eyes are a dead giveaway."

"Come on." Nancy nodded toward the door. "If I stop moving now, I'll collapse."

Nancy led Jake down the suite's narrow hallway to her room. Outside her door, though, she could hear her phone ringing. She didn't want Jake to hear anything in case it was about the party, so she started to stall. She dropped her keys, then fumbled with them in the lock.

"Don't you want to get that?" Jake asked about the ringing.

"The machine will," Nancy replied breezily. "It's not like I'm expecting any important calls or anything."

Jake eyed her strangely. "I see."

Inside the room, the answering machine was picking up. "Hi, this is Terry . . ." the message began.

Nancy froze.

She backed into Jake, grabbed him by the hand

and towed him back to the lounge. "I just remembered," she said, with no idea what to say next. The words "Kara's probably sleeping!" slipped miraculously off her tongue. "She had an early exam and was up studying all last night and asked me to be really quiet."

Jake obediently lowered himself into the soft couch. "A convoy of army trucks could drive through your room and not wake that girl up," he said.

Nancy shrugged. "I'm trying to be more considerate. We had a talk."

Jake eyed her incredulously. "Really."

"Really," Nancy insisted, trying to sound as guiltless as she could.

"Then I guess I'll wait here," he said, obviously confused and frustrated.

Well, if he wants a party, Nancy thought with a shrug, he'll just have to deal.

Then she remembered: he *doesn't* want a party.

Well, he will when he sees it, Nancy decided, and hurried back to her room.

Inside, of course, there was no sign of Kara. Her blankets were flung on the floor. The entire room was a wreck from the study-fest the night before.

Quickly, Nancy replayed Terry's message. He had special-ordered a leather notebook like his, engraved with Jake's name, and it was ready. She could come by and pick it up any time.

"Whew," Nancy said as she lowered herself onto her bed. "That was close."

Jake tried to push his way out of the couch, but flopped back down onto the spineless cushions. "Talking about needing new furniture," he muttered, his frustration only intensified by Nancy's weird behavior.

"What is her problem?" he wondered out loud.

Terry Schneider, he answered himself. That was him on the phone. I heard it. Which means—what?

Jake shrugged. What was the big deal? After all, they *were* in the film club together.

Then why didn't she want you to hear? He wondered darkly.

But before he could get any more depressed, the suite door opened and Stephanie tramped through. Not the Stephanie that Jake knew, but someone like her poor, more vulnerable sister.

She hadn't bothered with much makeup—just some eyeliner and a smear of lipstick. And her clothes, usually brassy and suggestive, were actually conservative, a pair of black wool slacks and a white sweater. And no jewelry.

Wow, Jake thought, maybe Nancy was right.

"Is Nancy around?" Stephanie asked.

"She'll be out in a second," Jake replied. "But are you okay?"

Stephanie sighed, worn out. "Don't ask."

"Nancy told me," Jake admitted. "It sounds weird."

Stephanie only nodded, as if she couldn't describe how she really felt.

"Stephanie!" Nancy strode in wearing fresh jeans and a white turtleneck under a bulky blue sweater, and carrying a full book bag over her shoulder.

Stephanie lowered herself onto the couch's arm. "After you left, Mrs. Caldwell called the police," she said dejectedly.

Nancy set her bag down. "Not about you?" she exclaimed.

"From what Nancy's told me, it doesn't sound as though they have any physical evidence," Jake asserted.

Stephanie only shrugged. "Who knows, but I saw a cop go into the personnel office and it's starting to get really scary. They can fire me, and I owe all this money—" Stephanie searched the room with her eyes, panicky.

Jake and Nancy exchanged worried glances. Jake felt actual sympathy toward Stephanie.

Getting accused of a crime is no picnic, he mused to himself.

And he should know. A few weeks earlier he and Nancy were in the wrong place, at the wrong time, and became suspects in an arson case. They were accused of trying to burn down a research lab on campus. The police were just about to arrest them when he and Nancy discovered the real culprit and forced her to confess.

"Hey, it's going to work out," Jake said soothingly.

"But how?" Stephanie asked desperately. "Nancy thinks Jonathan might be behind all this, which would be ultrabizarre." Stephanie searched Jake's eyes. "But what if he is? He likes Alice! And why use me? He also likes me! Nothing makes sense."

Jake nodded confidently. "Which is why you should relax. Everything'll be fine."

Stephanie just shook her head. "It's all too depressing."

Nancy stood next to Jake and squeezed his shoulder. "Thanks," she whispered in his ear.

As Nancy went over the events of the day with Stephanie, Jake tried for the second time to get out of the couch. He ended up sliding forward practically onto his knees to get up.

"Maybe we should get you guys a new couch while we're at it," he muttered.

Suddenly Nancy snapped her fingers. Her eyes lit up. "Hey," she said to Stephanie, "do you think you could use your employee discount on furniture?"

"Probably," Stephanie replied without enthusiasm. "But why are you suddenly talking furniture?"

"Because," Nancy said excitedly, "I think I

have a way to find out who's fouling up the shipments at Berrigan's."

"And nail the person who's framing me?" Stephanie asked hopefully.

"This I gotta see," Jake said.

Nancy snatched Jake's hand. "Oh, you will. Both of you. And right now."

"Me?" Stephanie asked, getting to her feet. "I don't want to go back there."

"It's your discount, isn't it?" Nancy told Stephanie.

Jake shook his head. "I don't get it."

But he did "get" the expression on Nancy's face. He knew her well enough to recognize one of her strokes of genius.

"Remember that new couch you guys need for your apartment?" she asked him. "Well, we're about to go buy you one. Come on, you guys, I'll explain in the car!"

"Ho, boy," Eileen cried as she staggered to the boathouse, grabbing at the stitch in her side. "Watch out, I'm going down."

Though he'd made it back to the boathouse only a few yards ahead of her, Emmet was already lying facedown on the grass by the edge of the parking lot. He rolled over and made some room and Eileen collapsed on the ground beside him.

"Okay," Emmet croaked. "I'll admit I'm winded."

"Yeah, me, too," Eileen gasped. "And I hope you realize you only beat me by a few steps."

"Plus the few you had on me with that surprise head start," Emmet pointed out.

"Hardly." Eileen managed to grin, still trying to catch her breath.

Eileen flopped onto her back, and for a few minutes, she and Emmet just lay there on the grass, staring up at the sky. There was no noise except the sound of the water lapping up against the boathouse docks and their own breathing in the chill air.

It's funny how peaceful this feels, Eileen thought, sneaking a glance in Emmet's direction. Not stressful the way it's been every other time we've been together.

"So," Emmet began, opening his eyes and turning his head toward her. Quickly, Eileen looked away, hoping she was still red enough from their race so that Emmet wouldn't notice her blush.

"It'll probably sound funny to say this," Emmet began, "but this is the best time I've had with you."

"Thanks." Eileen smiled. "My leg muscles are screaming in pain, and I'm on the verge of a heart attack."

"Hmm." Emmet nodded. "Nice, isn't it?"

Eileen laughed.

"You know, now that I'm totally exhausted," Emmet admitted, "it seems much easier to talk.

I don't have the energy to get into another disagreement."

"I never meant for that to be all we did with each other," Eileen said, wincing.

Emmet sighed. Then he rolled over on his side, facing her.

"I hated the way we left things," Emmet began. "I mean, if it's not going to work, it's just not going to work. But I don't like fighting like that. And I've been wanting to apologize for ruining the art opening for you."

"Thanks." Eileen smiled. "But it wasn't your fault. I can't deny it was embarrassing," she admitted, "but you were just being honest about how you felt. Believe it or not, I really do understand what you were saying. There *are* a lot of pretentious people in the arts."

Emmet cocked an eyebrow.

"Look, it's really a great thing that you're so unpretentious," Eileen went on. "I guess I should be glad you told me how you really felt instead of lying about it just to seem interested."

"But that's just it," Emmet replied earnestly. "I'm not *un*interested. You probably don't believe this, but I actually do like art. Maybe if I knew as much as you—you know, about color and all that stuff—I would appreciate what those guys were doing. But I just have to judge it on what I see. That's what art is to me. And I just didn't see much of anything that I could understand."

143

Eileen was surprised. What Emmet had said was really insightful. Obviously she hadn't given him credit for being thoughtful about his comments at the opening.

Emmet sighed and picked at the grass. "It's so funny. I mean, that I was trying so hard not to say the wrong things, and of course, the only things I said were wrong."

"No, Emmet," Eileen answered, shaking her head. She propped herself up on her elbow. "That's not really fair. I know you must have felt under a lot of pressure. And I guess most of my friends don't really expect a football player to say anything intelligent about art. I'm sorry if any of them—or me—made you feel like some stereotypical idiot jock."

"Look, it's all right," Emmet said. "It's all I'm known for. Football doesn't really lend itself to a great reputation as an art critic."

"No," Eileen disagreed. "It's not all right. Especially from me. Because I'm just as much of a jock as you are. I love getting up early for crew practice just as much as I love painting and drawing. And despite what I said about my impending heart attack"—she grinned—"it felt great to race with you just now."

"I guess we both needed to let off some steam," Emmet agreed.

"Yeah." Eileen nodded.

Emmet sighed. "I just don't understand it."

"What?" Eileen asked.

144

"How we can get along so well together when we're alone."

He was looking at her intently. Eileen caught her breath in her throat.

"I wish we could just stay here all afternoon by ourselves," Emmet said. "But now I'm afraid of what's going to happen when we get back to campus—and everyone else."

"But what can we do?" Eileen asked sadly. "Drop all of our friends?"

"Look," Emmet said, shyly reaching out and taking Eileen's hand. At his touch, Eileen's heart started to beat faster. "If it were that simple, I'd do it. I think it might be harder than that, but—" Emmet paused.

"But—?" Eileen asked.

"But I think it can work out," Emmet said. "At least, I'd like to keep trying. All we have to know and remember is this—" He met her eyes with his.

"And what's this?" Eileen asked softly.

"How we feel right now," Emmet said, smiling sweetly. "Just the two of us. You and me. And I think this is worth trying again."

Emmet squeezed her hand, and before she could even think about what she was doing, Eileen squeezed back.

"Me, too," she smiled shyly. "Only the next time we race, I'm going to be the one to win."

Emmet grinned. "You're on."

CHAPTER 12

"Trying to get anywhere around here at closing time is like trying to swim upriver," Nancy remarked as she, Stephanie, and Jake left special orders at Berrigan's and struggled through the crowd.

"Good couch," Stephanie said approvingly.

Jake had placed an order for a sleep sofa covered in a maroon, green, and black Southwestern-motif fabric.

"A little too good," Jake joked. "I'm worried about it with Nick and Dennis around."

"Let's take a break," Nancy said, pausing by the stairs that led down to the ordering and shipping department and the employee lockers.

"So we bought Jake a couch," Stephanie said impatiently. "Now what?"

"Now we watch and listen," Nancy said, scanning the store. "This morning Alice told me that she always spends the last hour of the day alone in her office, organizing the day's shipping receipts. With her behind a closed door, it seems like the perfect time for someone to fool around with any late orders that might have come in."

"Like the one for my couch?" Jake suggested.

Nancy could detect the glimmer of an approving smile at the corners of Stephanie's mouth. "Not bad," Stephanie said. "Though I'm surprised I didn't think of it," she added, barely audibly.

"It's mayhem," Jake said, eyeing the lines of last-minute customers snaking through the rows of merchandise.

"Here's the plan," Nancy said quickly. "With Alice busy, we go down to the loading dock—"

"And stop, look, and listen," Stephanie added.

Nancy nodded. "You got it. Let's go."

Stephanie led them down. The loading dock was deserted. Nancy and Jake took a seat behind the forklift, making sure to keep the merchandise shelves in sight, while Stephanie squatted behind a big box.

"You sure this is safe?" Jake whispered.

Nancy shrugged. "It's worth the chance. But Alice Woodward seems like a creature of habit to me. When she says she spends an hour in her office, I'd bet anything she spends an hour, no more, no less."

Nothing happened for a few minutes. It was getting cold. Nancy was afraid someone would see their breath rising behind the boxes.

Jake started rubbing his hands together. Stephanie mouthed—"This is boring."

Before Nancy could reply, she heard footsteps, and waving Stephanie down, ducked.

It was the salesperson who had sold them Jake's couch. She placed a stack of orders in a wire bin on the top shelf, then left.

Stephanie rolled her eyes, circling her finger in the air. Huge discovery.

She pulled out her pack of cigarettes and was about to light up when Nancy hissed. Jake drew a finger across his throat.

Stephanie looked ready to give up the whole plan when they all heard a second pair of footsteps.

"That's Jonathan Baur," Nancy whispered to Jake. She was impressed at the way Jonathan dressed. He had the posture of a model and the fashion taste of a designer. Nice leather lace-ups. Tall, dark, and sneaky. Perfect for Stephanie.

"But why's he acting so suspiciously?" she wondered aloud.

Jonathan had stopped in front of the shelves and was looking left and right, then behind him, then left and right again, seeing if the coast was clear.

Nancy threw a glance Stephanie's way. She was watching Jonathan like a hawk. She was probably wondering the same thing and hoping it wasn't what it looked like.

Then Nancy's heart dropped. Looking around him again, Jonathan had grabbed the stack of orders and pocketed them, and started to walk away quickly.

But before Nancy knew what was happening, Stephanie sprang out from behind the boxes. "Wait!" Nancy called.

But it was too late. Stephanie was in Jonathan's face, pointing at his pocket bulging with the orders, her face pinched with angry accusation. "What are you doing!"

Bess, Brian, and Casey were huddled around a small table in the Underground, eating burgers.

"Only fifteen minutes before rehearsal," Brian reminded them, shoving a pile of french fries onto his hamburger.

"Ugh." Casey wrinkled her nose. "What are you doing, trying out for a fast-food commercial or something? Don't be so inventive with your food. It's bad for the digestion."

"I'll tell you what's bad for the digestion," Bess said, suddenly hiding her eyes. "Chronic embarrassment! Look who's here."

"Alan," Brian said.

"And Jeanne Glasseburg," Casey added happily.

"Is she going to sit in on the rehearsals, too?" Bess moaned. "It's bad enough that I made such a moron of myself in front of her. I'd at least like to rehearse more before she sees my one-act."

"I thought you stopped obsessing over your little performance," Brian said.

Bess shrugged. "Paul made me feel a little better, but really, what does he know about acting? And he wasn't even there."

Bess stared across the room at her acting professor and the famous acting coach. There was no use trying to pretend she hadn't looked like a fool. She was more sure than ever that she'd never get into that acting class.

Just then Alan Farber and Jeanne Glasseburg glanced at their table. After a private word, they headed over.

"Wow," Brian said. "Looks like they're coming here."

"Probably to say hello to you," Bess said to Casey. "You're the only real actress here, after all."

But when they reached the table, Jeanne Glasseburg gave Casey only a nod hello and stopped right in front of Bess!

"Here she is," Alan said.

Here who is? Bess wondered, mortified. The amateur who embarrassed herself in front of a roomful of students and one very famous acting coach?

"Of course," Ms. Glasseburg said. A small smile played around her lips. "Bess, isn't it?"

"Yes, Bess Marvin," Bess replied, keeping her

eyes down. She hoped she wasn't as red as she felt. But when she glanced at Casey and Brian, she could tell from their horrified expressions how badly she was blushing.

"So, Bess," Ms. Glasseburg went on, "I caught your . . . well . . . presentation the other night."

"It wasn't exactly a presentation," Bess said quickly. "I was just fooling around—"

"Theater is very serious business," Ms. Glasseburg said, interrupting her.

And obviously I'm not serious enough, Bess finished the thought silently, dropping her head in shame.

"Which is why it always needs a good healthy dose of fun," Ms. Glasseburg added.

Bess couldn't believe her ears. When she looked up, Jeanne Glasseburg was actually grinning at her. Her severe looks had softened. Her eyes seemed to pierce Bess with goodwill.

"It's a lesson lots of actors and actresses never learn," Ms. Glasseburg continued. "It's easy to bore an audience and hard to make them smile. Let me tell you a secret. Acting seriously is one thing," she said, leaning over their table. "But taking yourself too seriously is another."

She looked at Bess approvingly. "It's great to see a young actress unafraid of comedy and laughter."

Bess's jaw dropped.

"So"—Ms. Glasseburg grinned—"I'm looking forward to seeing how you perform in the one-act plays. You have the kind of personality I'd love to be able to bring into my class next semester."

Bess couldn't answer—until Brian elbowed her in the side.

"Thank you," she managed to croak as the two adults turned away.

Bess was still in so much shock, she barely registered Alan's throwing her a wink.

"Bess?" Casey said. "Bess? Bess are you okay? You should breathe now, you know."

"She's going to faint," Brian said nervously.

"Did—did she . . ." Bess stammered, turning back to her friends. "Did Jeanne Glasseburg just . . . *my* sense of humor . . . the right kind of *personality?*"

"Yes!" Casey crowed, grabbing Bess by the shoulders. "Jeanne Glasseburg loves you!"

Bess wanted to laugh. Or shout. Or cry.

She couldn't believe it. She hadn't ruined her chances after all!

"What do you mean, what am I doing?" Jonathan was objecting to Stephanie. "What are *you* doing?" He threw Nancy and Jake a suspicious stare. "And who are you?"

"My question first," Stephanie insisted, her eyes blazing. "What about those shipping orders?"

"What, these?" Jonathan replied, holding up the stack of papers.

"Wait a second, you guys," Nancy cut in.

"Who *are* you?" Jonathan shot back.

"My friends," Stephanie said. "They're trying to help me."

Nancy looked worriedly up the hall toward Alice's office. "Let's just calm down a second," she suggested.

Stephanie snatched the papers out of Jonathan's hand. "I *am* calm!"

Jonathan smiled wryly, looking at Stephanie as if he liked what he saw. "No, you're not," he said coolly. "You want to punch me."

The papers in Stephanie's hand were shaking. "Why were you changing these orders, Jonathan?" she asked point-blank.

Jonathan raised an eyebrow and considered them all. "You mean you were laying a trap and I walked into it?"

Everyone nodded.

"Well, all I can say is, nice try," Jonathan said, amused, "but you've got the wrong guy. As a matter of fact, we're on the same team."

He gazed at Stephanie, cleared his throat, and went on. "Actually, I was always pretty sure you weren't behind all these problems. And maybe I didn't want you to be. There were others who seemed suspicious. So I've been going over the shipping orders when no one's around, checking for anything that doesn't look right."

Nancy noticed that Stephanie's expression had slipped from disappointment and shock to thankfulness. She was holding out the receipts to Jonathan.

"Then I compare the merchandise to what's on the order," Jonathan went on, taking the receipts back. "Maybe the handwriting doesn't fit or something. I have no idea how this is all happening, so I've been looking for anything weird, really."

"But why were you acting so sneaky just now?" Nancy asked.

Jonathan thumbed back over his shoulder toward Alice's office. "Because she wouldn't like it," he said quietly. "She thinks it's her job, because it's her department." He looked apologetically at Stephanie. "She's kind of biased. I'm not."

Stephanie sniffed. They stood in silence for a second, taking it all in.

"But what about that paper you had Stephanie sign yesterday?" Jake chimed in.

"Yeah," Stephanie said, a little softer now. "That was the only thing I signed all day, and I didn't really look at it."

Nancy shrugged. "You can see how we'd think you gave her a shipping order to sign instead, so that the mistake could be pinned on her later."

Chuckling softly, Jonathan shook his head. "I'd probably think the same thing. But I wasn't even the one who noticed the order. Someone else did when she was handing in her own receipts. I was only the messenger."

"Who was it?" Nancy wanted to know.

"Kristin St. Clair," Jonathan replied.

"Kristin?" Stephanie exclaimed. "Kristin wouldn't do this to me. We're friends."

Jonathan was nodding in agreement. "And she's an excellent employee."

Stephanie nodded. "Yeah, she is. It runs in her family. She's just like her dad was at Dancor's."

Nancy's throat tightened with the sudden realization. The montage of photos and cards behind Alice's desk flashed before her eyes. Looming large was the picture with Alice standing in front of the entrance to Dancor's.

Eyes wide, mouth agape, Nancy snapped her fingers. "That's it!"

CHAPTER 13

Nancy, Jake, Stephanie, and now Jonathan were sitting on the back end of the forklift, out of view of the central loading dock. The day's shipping orders were returned to the bin on the shelf. It was a quarter to seven. Alice's hour was up in fifteen minutes.

"My life is a mess right at this moment," Stephanie said. "It's too cold, and this forklift is hard. I haven't done a stitch of homework in a week, I'm about to lose my job, and I just found out it's because of someone I thought really liked me."

Jonathan shrugged. "Sorry."

To Stephanie's own surprise, she graciously accepted his sympathy. "Thanks," she said. "I appreciate your vote of confidence."

"Look, I'm not positive it's Kristin," Nancy said. "It's just a hunch."

Stephanie pictured Kristin's pretty face, and how she was the one who had welcomed her to the Berrigan's staff and introduced her around the store. "I can't believe it. Why would she want to ruin the store's reputation?"

Nancy shook her head. "I don't think that's what she's trying to do. Listen, there's a picture of Alice standing in front of Dancor's on her bulletin board. I think she used to work there," Nancy said.

"She did," replied Jonathan. "She started in retail there."

"Well, think about it, you guys," Nancy said.

Stephanie looked up to see Nancy staring hard at her.

"Stephanie, remember how Kristin was saying her dad was fired after working there for so long? Didn't you detect a note of bitterness in her voice? Like Dancor's was the most evil place on earth."

Stephanie thought about that conversation with Kristin and Pam the other day. Now that she thought about it, Kristin's voice had sounded a little tight when she was telling the story.

"Maybe Alice had something to do with Mr. St. Clair getting fired," Nancy suggested.

Stephanie was nodding. "And Kristin might want some kind of revenge. I get it!"

Stephanie shrugged. She pictured Alice's face twisting with anger and heard again the echoing harsh tones of Alice's accusing voice.

"Who can blame Kristin?" Stephanie wondered aloud. "I can't."

Jonathan's brow furrowed. "Even if she used you to get her revenge?" he asked.

But Stephanie didn't have time to respond. She whirled at the sound of footsteps on the loading dock.

Crawling forward, Stephanie peered around the edge of the forklift. Someone was going through the stack of receipts on the shelf. Stephanie couldn't mistake the curly brown hair or the fashionable dress or the familiar fishnet stockings. It was Kristin!

"Not yet," Nancy was whispering behind her.

Oh, I know, Stephanie thought to herself, suddenly surging with composure and purpose. For the first time in the last five long days, she felt in control. And instead of feeling confused and sorry for herself, she felt angry.

Jonathan's right, Stephanie thought. Maybe Alice deserves a little revenge. But Kristin was using *me!*

"Look," Jake whispered.

But Stephanie had already seen the pen in Kristin's hand and seen Kristin look surreptitiously over her shoulder.

Now the pen came down on a receipt. Kristin crossed something out, then wrote something in its place!

*   *   *

Ginny was in a daze as she returned to suite 301 that evening. She hadn't had a chance to talk to anyone about her conversation with Ray the night before. Unfortunately it was all she could think about, and she'd been fighting back tears all day. Her stomach was in knots, and her head was pounding.

"What am I going to do if Ray drops out?" she wondered out loud as she opened the suite door. "What happens to *us?*"

When Ginny walked into the suite's lounge, Kara, Casey, Liz, and Reva were in the middle of a hot game of casino. Ginny was so relieved to see them that she almost burst into tears.

"What's up with you?" Reva asked, looking up as Ginny came in. "You don't look so hot."

Ginny just shook her head. She dropped her bag and sat down on the couch.

"Ginny?" Reva leaned forward anxiously. "What is it?"

"You look awful," Liz said, draping an arm around her roommate's shoulder.

"I don't know what I'm going to do," Ginny said, shaking her head. "You know how Ray and the Beat Poets got this record deal with Pacific Records?"

"Like we could forget that people we actually know are probably going to end up in the next Lollapalooza tour?" Kara asked.

"Well, last night Ray told me he might quit

school!" Ginny looked at her friends, her eyes wide with worry.

Casey grimaced. "Wow!"

"I don't know what to say to change his mind," Ginny said. "It's like he's already decided."

"But a record company deal," Kara replied, shaking her head. "It would be kind of crazy to ask him to give up a chance like that."

"So instead he gives up the chance at an education?" Liz asked.

"And gives up on me?" Ginny added softly.

"No way," Reva argued. "Ray *loves* you. You are the coolest couple. Anyone can tell that just by looking at you guys. He didn't tell you he'd want to break up, did he?"

"No," Ginny admitted. "But he'd have to be in California a lot. What kind of relationship could we have?"

Casey cleared her throat.

"Oh, Case, I'm sorry," Ginny said. "I don't mean that you and Charley don't have a relationship. But it's totally different for you. You guys have been together for years. And now you're engaged. But a recording deal? How can I possibly compete with that?"

"Despite the fact that quitting school doesn't sound like the smartest thing to do, no matter what's going on with you two," Reva said firmly.

Casey nodded. "I'm with you one hundred percent. I've been there, and even *I've* decided that my education is too important to give up completely."

"But, you guys," Kara shook her head. "Look, I'll feel bad for Ginny if Ray leaves, but we're talking about a *record* deal. That means records, and CDs and videos and stuff. It's the biggest break he could get!"

"I know, I know," Ginny moaned. "And I'm trying to be supportive. I know how amazing the record deal is. But I also know how important an education is. I just don't want him to throw away his whole future on a whim."

"But is music just a whim to Ray?" Casey asked, confused. "I thought he was totally serious about it."

Ginny sighed. What could she say? Casey was right. Ray was serious about his music. Serious and good. That's why he was actually thinking of dropping out of school.

Maybe I'm the one who enjoys music as a whim, she admitted.

Writing songs with Ray had been fun and had allowed her to imagine another side of herself, but she would never drop out of school to become a full-time musician.

"Maybe you're right," Ginny said sadly. "Playing music is what he really wants to be doing. I guess I'm just worried about him rushing into something."

And rushing away from me, Ginny added silently.

"Well, opportunities like this don't come along for every band," Reva pointed out.

But Ginny had stopped hearing clearly.

Someone was saying, "Let him follow his dream."

But what about my dream? Ginny wanted to ask. The one that includes Wilder *and* Ray?

Ginny swallowed hard as she tried to imagine Wilder without him.

She shivered. It was just too awful to think about.

But Wilder without Ray was looming ahead of her like the inescapable future. Days and nights without Ray.

Life without Ray.

"Hey!" Jonathan Baur shouted.

Nancy and the others bolted out from behind the forklift. Confronted, Kristin's beautiful face froze into a mask of fear. The papers in her hand began to shake. The pen dropped.

Nancy knew she was right about her, but she also knew that this wasn't the end of the story. There had to be more. Much more.

"Kristin, how could you?" Stephanie asked.

Kristin opened her mouth to speak, but she saw something out of the corner of her eye and stopped.

"How could she what?"

Everyone turned. Alice Woodward was standing in the doorway to the loading dock. "What are you all doing?" she snapped. "No one's allowed back here after closing."

"I think Kristin has something to tell you," Nancy said quickly. "Don't you?"

Alice turned to Nancy. "You're the research student from this morning," she said, confused. "What are you doing here? And Stephanie and Jonathan? And who's this other man?" Alice pointed at Jake.

Nancy blushed. "I'm sorry, Ms. Woodward, but I'm not writing a paper. I'm a friend of Stephanie's. I was just trying to see if I could figure out what was going on."

"You were spying?" Alice glared at them all, hands on hips. "Jonathan, what is all this? I'm going to call human resources," she declared, and turned.

But Kristin broke her silence. "Wait . . . Alice," she called her back.

Alice whirled. "What is it, Kristin?" she asked impatiently.

Kristin started to say something, then stopped. "Nothing," she said uncertainly.

"What do you mean, *nothing?*" Stephanie cried.

Alice pointed at Stephanie. "You're really in trouble!"

"I don't think so," Jonathan cut in.

That seemed to make Alice pause. Narrowing her eyes, she crossed her arms. "Will someone tell me what's going on?"

All eyes were on Kristin, and slowly, gradually, she seemed to wither beneath them.

"All the trouble that's been happening in your department isn't Stephanie's fault," Jonathan said quietly but firmly.

"Well, thank you," Stephanie muttered, throwing up her arms in exasperation. "Finally!"

"But if it isn't Stephanie, then who is it?" Alice wanted to know.

"It's Kristin!" Stephanie blurted.

Wide-eyed, Alice snorted and shook her head. "Kristin? *Kristin!* She's the finest employee in this store. You've really gone too far now."

Nancy noticed that Kristin was looking around at everybody, her lips beginning to tremble.

Nancy stepped over to her. "Why don't you tell her," she prodded quietly. "We know there has to be a good reason."

At first Kristin clenched her jaw defiantly, but just as quickly, she let herself go and seemed to soften, as though she'd just figured it all out herself.

Her voice lowered to a whisper. "I'm the one you've been looking for, Alice."

"You?" Alice asked in disbelief. She threw an uncertain glance at Stephanie, then stepped toward Kristin. "You better explain what's going on here, young lady."

Kristin lifted her face, and Nancy could tell from her expression that she was caught between anger and sadness.

"I've been fouling up the orders," she confessed.

From the corner of her eye, Nancy could see Stephanie and Jonathan looking at Kristin, confused, relieved, and sad.

"Because—" Kristin went on, locking her gaze on Alice. "My father was fired at Dancor's."

Alice looked confused. "Your father? I don't know what you're talking about."

"Because of *you!*" Kristin said. "My father lost his job. Frank St. Clair? He hadn't been feeling well, and he made a mistake with the sales receipts one day. Just once!"

She leveled an accusing glare at Alice. "He was Dancor's employee of the year *ten* times, and you had him fired," she said coldly. "He'd worked there since before you were born, and you just came in and treated him as if he was nothing, an insect."

Alice looked off into the middle distance, then nodded with recognition. "Frank St. Clair. I *do* remember him. But, Kristin, you have to understand, it wasn't my decision to fire him. That order came from higher up. I was like your dad, just trying to do my job the best I could."

Kristin wouldn't hear it. She choked down a sob. "He always blamed you," she seethed. "And then he couldn't find another job, and he got even *sicker.* All he mentioned was Alice Woodward, Alice Woodward, half his age and coming in and just firing him."

"Kristin—" Stephanie tried to cut in.

"I had no idea you were employed here when I started working," Kristin continued over Stephanie's protest. "Then I came in and saw you sitting behind your desk, and your nameplate in front of you. I'd heard your name so many times over the past few years, and I *despised* you!" Tears began to fall. "That's when I decided to do it."

Alice looked upset. "But it wasn't me," she insisted. "I'm sorry about your dad, Kristin, but it wasn't me that had him fired. I was just the messenger."

"And it wasn't me, either," Stephanie interrupted. "Whatever you had going on with Alice, you had no right to drag me into it. You set me up, Kristin! You used me!"

Kristin slowly swung her head toward Stephanie. "Sorry, Stephanie," she said, her voice thick with emotion. "You were convenient."

"Convenient!" Stephanie replied, aghast. "I thought we were friends!"

"It's too bad you resorted to that," Nancy spoke up. "You dragged the entire store into this. You set up someone who liked you. You made it a lot worse than it had to be."

Alice was nodding. "You should have talked to me," she said mournfully.

"And what would you have said?" Kristin sneered. " 'Sorry I ruined your father's life'?"

"No," Alice replied calmly. "Maybe what happened to your father could have been handled better, but it wasn't my decision. I would have told you that you were blaming the wrong person."

Jonathan had broken away from the group.

"Where are you going?" Alice demanded, her authority returned to her voice.

"I'm calling Mrs. Caldwell," he replied.

Kristin lowered herself onto an overturned crate and suddenly began to sob. Alice stepped over and put her arm around her, not saying a word.

"I hate you," Kristin said through her tears, as if she was trying to convince herself. As if she didn't believe it anymore.

Nancy felt Jake's hand crawl into hers. "Wow," he said.

Nancy could see Stephanie shaking her head. "It's okay," she told her. "It's over now."

Stephanie turned her face. Her eyes were wet. "Thanks, Nancy. You saved my life."

Nancy gave Stephanie's arm an affectionate squeeze. "Not your life"—she smiled—"just your credit cards."

CHAPTER 14

Nine o'clock Wednesday night, Nancy was sitting in her cubicle at the *Wilder Times* office, tapping out a song on her desk. She was eyeing the phone and then the door, a self-satisfied smile playing across her face. The office was deserted. The only sound she could hear was her heart thumping. Her palms were sweaty.

She heard footsteps on the stairs outside, and suddenly snapped into action. She quickly ruffled a few papers, tossed some red pencils here and there, and sat squarely at her desk, staring unhappily at her darkened computer monitor.

"Okay, okay, so now I'm here," Jake was muttering as he burst through the doors. "Where's the patient?"

He was breathing heavily. Nancy had to laugh

when she saw he wasn't wearing his cowboy boots. He had his slippers on.

"Oh, did I wake you?" she asked unrepentantly.

Jake narrowed his eyes. "You know you did. From my post-all-nighter, post-exam nap."

They were all finishing up their three days of exams or writing papers, and were in recovery mode.

Nancy swallowed, gripping her desk, struggling to keep herself from smiling.

"Sorry," she said. She tried to add a touch of panic to her voice. "For some reason my computer just won't go on, and I promised Gail I'd have all these articles redlined by tomorrow morning!"

Jake squatted next to Nancy and looked at the computer. Then he peered under the desk. He came out slowly, shaking his head.

"Um, Nance?"

"Yes?" Nancy asked innocently.

"It wasn't plugged in. Try it now."

Obediently Nancy flipped the switch, and her computer flickered to life. "Oh."

Jake stood. "Nancy, what's wrong with you?" he asked her directly. "Where's the self-sufficient, straight-talking Nancy I went to the movies with and walked back to her dorm last Thursday night?"

Nancy pulled Jake down on her lap by his belt loop and planted a warm kiss on his neck.

"Right here," she said seductively. She kissed

him again. "And here." She lifted his hand and kissed his fingers. "And here, and here—"

Tonight she couldn't afford to take no for an answer. Not after everything she'd planned. She'd made sure to wear something that might give Jake a few irresistible ideas: a skintight black lambswool mock-turtleneck and her tightest, softest jeans.

Jake lifted her chin. "What about your articles?"

Nancy shrugged. "What about them?"

Jake eyed her suspiciously, then broke into a smile. "It's your funeral," he said, and kissed her deeply. "Gail's going to have you for breakfast."

His lips played across her face, kissing her eyelids, her cheeks. He nibbled on her ear.

For a second the entire plan drifted out of Nancy's mind, and she was happy back in Jake's arms. They hadn't been together like this in days, and the days had felt like years. . . .

"I'm wild for you," she started to say when the phone rang and abruptly punctured the mood.

"Don't answer it," Jake whispered.

Nancy almost didn't. Then she remembered.

She thought quickly. "It might be Gail, with orders," she said.

"Hello?"

Nancy listened for a second, then handed the phone to Jake. "It's for you. It's Nick."

"You've got to be kidding me!" Jake cried. "The first time I have you to myself in a week and—" He yelled loudly into the receiver, "Tell him I'm not here!"

Nancy bit the inside of her cheek to keep from laughing. "He says it's important."

Grumbling, Jake snatched at the phone. "What!" He listened for a second, then slammed it down. "I hate that store!" he cried.

"What is it?"

"Nick says that the Berrigan's guys actually showed up five minutes ago. At *nine o'clock* at night! But get this. They delivered a reclining chair with a paisley pattern, not a couch."

"Why can't Nick just send it back?"

"They won't talk to Nick about it," Jake said. "They have to talk to me since it's my order."

"I *liked* that couch," Nancy complained.

"Okay, fine," Jake said, getting up. "We're going." He straightened his shirt. "But I want a rain check," he insisted.

Nancy circled her arms around his neck. "Anytime, anyplace—almost."

Nancy followed Jake through the office door, out into the cool night, and across the quad. She could hear him muttering to himself all the way about stupid department stores and screwed-up orders.

Just you wait, she thought gleefully to herself. Just you wait and see.

Matching Jake stride for stride, she felt overwhelming love for him. She'd do anything for him. She'd never tell another lie.

She just had to get through the next five minutes.

"This is so great!" Bess cried as she and Paul pushed their way into Jake's apartment. "This place filled up with people in ten minutes!"

The place was already packed with people for Jake's surprise party. Bess saw that everyone from Nancy's suite was there. She spotted George and Will stuck across the room, and dragged Paul through the crowd to them.

"Hey!" George cried, grabbing her cousin in a hug. "I got the message you left about that acting coach. Excellent!"

"Thanks." Bess smiled. "Good thing we had a party to come to."

"And this is going to be some party," Will agreed. "If we manage to actually say, 'Surprise,' when he gets here."

"I can't believe Jake doesn't suspect anything." Bess shook her head.

"Especially with all these people," Paul muttered, looking around the apartment.

"Leave it to Nancy." George chuckled. "She didn't forget anyone. I think she would have invited his old high school teachers if she could have found out who they were."

"I know everyone from Thayer," Bess said. "But who are all the other people?"

"Some newspaper people," Will said. "And people from that animal rescue league he's in."

"The guy isn't short on friends, that's for sure," George joked.

"He just blackmails them," Nick Dimartini interjected straight-faced as he passed them with a tray of food. "They know that if they aren't his friends, he'll write nasty things about them in the paper."

"Yep, a great guy, just as we suspected," Bess joked back.

"Hey, there she is! The young starlet Jeanne Glasseburg's got her famous eyes on!"

All of a sudden, Bess was surrounded by Casey, Brian, and Brian's friend, Chris.

"Oh, you most supreme and all-powerful actress-in-a-leading-comic-role," Brian teased, "share your humorous insights with me so that I, too, might have a chance at getting into the mighty Glasseburg's spring acting seminar!"

Bess knew she was blushing, but didn't care.

"Well, no matter what Jeanne Glasseburg said, I want to rehearse a lot before our one-acts," she said sincerely. "Now I *really* need to do a great job. Especially if she's going to be expecting something wonderful from me."

"Let's get together tomorrow afternoon," Brian said.

"Perfect!" Casey replied excitedly.

"And you'll bless us with your presence, of course," Brian added, grinning at Bess.

173

"Oh, I don't know." Bess tossed her blond hair back over her shoulder and sniffed.

"She'll be there," Paul answered. "But only after *I* feel sufficiently blessed." He grabbed Bess around the waist and picked her up.

"Are you feeling ignored?" Bess teased, gazing happily into Paul's eyes.

"Not anymore," Paul said, and he grinned.

"Oh, look"—Bess pointed across the crowded room—"Eileen and Emmet."

"They're actually having a great time together." Paul smiled.

"I'm so happy for her," Bess said. She watched for a few minutes as Eileen and Emmet stood talking quietly to each other, heads bent close together so they could hear over the noise of the crowd.

"They look cute," Bess decided.

"Almost as cute as you," Paul replied, not taking his eyes off Bess even for a second. He leaned down and wrapped her in a warm hug.

Bess gazed around the room full of her friends over Paul's shoulder. Then she stepped back and looked up at Paul. She was falling in love with him. Maybe she already had. There was no doubt about how happy she was.

She circled Paul's waist with her arms. "Life can't get better than this," she said, squeezing him hard. She lifted her face for a kiss.

"But it will," Paul replied lovingly.

"I can't wait."

* * *

Stephanie zeroed in on a plate of spinach pastry-dough things and snatched up two, then grabbed a third.

"Whoa, there!" Casey exclaimed. "I thought you only ate apples and chocolate."

Stephanie waved blithely. "Not anymore."

"You're a changed woman." Casey nodded.

Stephanie peered down the length of her nose. "Don't exaggerate." Then she and Casey broke into gales of laughter. "To tell you the truth, I've never been so hungry in my life! The last two days, all I've done is eat."

Casey laid a sympathetic hand on her shoulder. "I'm glad everything worked out."

"Thanks," Stephanie mumbled as Casey drifted away from her. She knew Casey hadn't heard her. But that didn't matter. It felt good just to say it. She'd said "Thanks" more in the last two days than she had in her entire life.

But there was one more thing she had to say.

She straightened the hem of her slinky black dress, smacked her bloodred lips together, ran her fingers through her long black hair, and picked her way through the crowd right toward Pam.

She was talking with her boyfriend, Jamal. When she saw Stephanie coming, her eyes hardened.

"Friends?" Stephanie asked, and held out a hand.

Pam took Stephanie's hand warily. "I guess," she said, sounding unconvinced.

Stephanie cleared her throat. "I'm sorry I accused you of being behind what happened at the store," she said directly.

Pam didn't reply. She just looked shocked. Maybe it was the noise.

"Sorry," Stephanie repeated.

Pam blinked. "It's okay," she said, her eyes softening. "I mean, I accept."

Stephanie rolled her eyes. "Good," she said, relieved. "Because I like working with you."

"Me, too. Wow, Steph, this thing really got to you, huh?"

Stephanie shrugged. She was about to say something clever and casual, then stopped herself and nodded. "It sure did. And the funny thing is, it only took me about five minutes to stop hating Kristin for what she did. Actually, I felt sorry for her."

"They're going to fire her?" Pam asked.

Stephanie nodded. "And the only way Berrigan's wouldn't press criminal charges was if she agreed to therapy."

Pam nodded. "They always give everyone a second chance," she said.

Stephanie thought about that as she drifted back into the party. A second chance. Now she felt as if she had hers.

Stephanie scanned the crowd.

Casey sidled up to her and handed her a glass.

"Pretty impressive supply of gorgeous men," she said. "And available, too. Just like shooting fish in a barrel."

Stephanie stared at her roommate. "Didn't I hear something about you and an engagement?"

Casey waved. "Is looking a crime?"

Stephanie laughed ruefully. "It could be."

Casey shrugged sadly. "You know the rule: look but don't touch. . . . But, hey, what about you? There are about twenty guys in this room staring at you right now. Which one do you want?"

Stephanie's eyes hopped from face to handsome face. Piercing eyes, muscular arms, washboard stomachs, snappy dressers. She had her pick. They were all there.

She didn't want any of them.

All she could think about was the phone call she'd received from Jonathan the night before. He'd called to ask if she was okay. And he'd called for another reason: maybe they could catch a movie sometime. He wanted to get to know her better.

He wants to get to know me, Stephanie thought to herself. So he does like me.

Usually when it came to guys, Stephanie's only interest was the thrill of the hunt. She liked it that way. She came, she saw, she conquered, she was gone. No mess, no fuss, no commitment, no hurt.

But what she felt now was a flutter of actual fear. And that was a first.

You're in trouble, girl, she realized. You like that man. You care about him. And if he ever says no to you, it's going to hurt.

Mess, she considered. Commitment.

It sounded hopelessly scary.

So, Stephanie Keats, she asked herself, what are you going to do?

When Jake turned the corner onto Waterman Street, he stopped dead in his tracks.

"What is it?" Nancy asked.

"They already left!" he cried, pointing to the curb in front of his apartment complex. There was no sign of a Berrigan's truck. "I can't believe they didn't even wait! They'd better not have left that chair," he threatened.

He swore he heard Nancy laugh. He whirled. "What's so funny?"

Nancy held up her hands in mock surrender. "Sorry," she said, "but you look so funny. You're so mad, and you're wearing your slippers!"

Jake felt his frustration slipping away.

"It's just a couch, Jake," Nancy said with a giggle. "It'll be back tomorrow."

"Okay, you win," he said. So it wasn't his night. At least he still had Nancy to be with. That is if she didn't get weird on him again.

Nancy hooked her arm through his. "Let's go up."

Halfway up the stairs, though, Jake stopped. He thought he heard something.

"Come on," Nancy said, tugging on Jake's arm.

"What's the hurry?"

"I'm cold," Nancy complained, and started dragging Jake.

"I thought I heard something," Jake started to say.

With a ferocious pull, Jake found himself being yanked up the stairs and in through his apartment door.

It was dark. And it smelled like food.

Stumbling, Jake was laughing and gripping all at once. "Cut it out!" he yelled. "I can't see."

Suddenly the lights came on.

"Surprise!" everyone cried. A roomful of blurry faces was smiling and laughing and yelling at him all at once.

Jake blinked. People were patting him on the shoulder. Girls were kissing him on the cheeks.

A huge banner, *Chicago Herald: Congratulations Jake!* hung across the living-room wall. Balloons and streamers were everywhere. A big cake sat on a table with lots of great-looking food.

"Way to go!"

"Next stop, Pulitzer prize!"

Somewhere in his brain, Jake knew he wasn't supposed to like surprise parties. He didn't like the attention. It was embarrassing.

But as he looked around the packed apartment and saw all the great friends who'd come to congratulate him, Jake realized surprise parties were terrific!

Jake swallowed hard.

"I think for the first time in recent memory, Jake Collins is speechless!" Nancy laughed. Everyone was hysterical.

Jake spotted Terry Schneider in the crowd. "You!" Jake laughed, pointing. "You were in on this."

Terry smiled crookedly. "Barely. It was all Nancy."

"Hey!" Jake reached out to grab Nancy. He pulled her toward him.

"Surprised?" Nancy asked, her eyes twinkling with mischief.

"I am very surprised," Jake admitted.

"Well, you didn't make it easy," Nancy said. "But I did it."

"And you're so proud of yourself," he teased. "I can tell."

"Only a little less proud than I am of you," Nancy smiled, leaning forward. She kissed him sweetly, clamping his face in her soft hands.

"Now I just have one more little surprise," she said mysteriously. She reached down and pulled a package out from her bag. "For you," she said, handing it to Jake. "So you're never without a place to put those brilliant thoughts."

"A present too?" Jake asked, overwhelmed.

Quickly, Jake tore off the wrapping paper. He held the gift for a while before he could speak.

It was beautiful and perfect. The leather-bound notebook with his name on it was the best present he'd ever gotten. He turned it over and over in his hands.

"Do you like it?" Nancy asked, biting her lip worriedly.

"Like it?" Jake shook his head. He stepped close to her and put his lips to her ear.

"Somehow the word *like* is never enough when it comes to you," he whispered. "It's incredible."

"Every big-time reporter should have one," Nancy added with a nod.

"No, every big-time reporter should have a girlfriend as wonderful as you," Jake growled, pulling Nancy into his arms. "What I really want to know is, how did I get to be so lucky?"

Now your younger brothers or sisters
can take a walk down Fear Street....

R·L·STINE'S
GHOSTS of FEAR STREET ®

1 Hide and Shriek	52941-2/$3.99
2 Who's Been Sleeping in My Grave?	52942-0/$3.99
3 Attack of the Aqua Apes	52943-9/$3.99
4 Nightmare in 3-D	52944-7/$3.99
5 Stay Away From the Tree House	52945-5/$3.99
6 Eye of the Fortuneteller	52946-3/$3.99
7 Fright Knight	52947-1/$3.99
8 The Ooze	52948-X/$3.99
9 Revenge of the Shadow People	52949-8/$3.99
10 The Bugman Lives	52950-1/$3.99
11 The Boy Who Ate Fear Street	00183-3/$3.99
12 Night of the Werecat	00184-1/$3.99
13 How to be a Vampire	00185-X/$3.99

A MINSTREL® BOOK

FEAR STREET® SAGA

Collector's Edition

Including
The Betrayal
The Secret
The Burning

R·L·STINE

Why do so many terrifying things happen on Fear Street? Discover the answer in this special collector's edition of the *Fear Street Saga* trilogy, something no Fear Street fan should be without.

Special bonus: the Fear Street family tree, featuring all those who lived—and died—under the curse of the Fears.

Coming in mid-October 1996

From Archway Paperbacks
Published by Pocket Books

POCKET
B O O K S

1233